SLEEPER CODE

Also by Tom Sniegoski

Sleeper Agenda

SLEEPER CODE

PART I
IN THE **SLEEPER** *CONSPIRACY*

TOM SNIEGOSKI

razor
bill

Sleeper Code

RAZORBILL

Published by the Penguin Group
Penguin Young Readers Group
345 Hudson Street, New York, New York 10014, U.S.A.
Penguin Group (USA) Inc., 375 Hudson Street, New York,
New York 10014, U.S.A.
Penguin Group (Canada), 90 Eglinton Avenue, Suite 700, Toronto,
Ontario, Canada M4P 2Y3 (a division of Pearson Penguin Canada Inc.)
Penguin Books Ltd, 80 Strand, London WC2R 0RL, England
Penguin Ireland, 25 St Stephen's Green, Dublin 2, Ireland
(a division of Penguin Books Ltd)
Penguin Group (Australia), 250 Camberwell Road, Camberwell,
Victoria 3124, Australia (a division of Pearson Australia Group Pty Ltd)
Penguin Books India Pvt Ltd, 11 Community Centre, Panchsheel Park,
New Delhi - 110 017, India
Penguin Group (NZ), Cnr Airborne and Rosedale Roads, Albany,
Auckland 1310, New Zealand (a division of Pearson New Zealand Ltd)
Penguin Books (South Africa) (Pty) Ltd, 24 Sturdee Avenue,
 Rosebank, Johannesburg 2196, South Africa

Penguin Books Ltd, Registered Offices: 80 Strand, London WC2R 0RL, England

10 9 8 7 6 5 4 3 2 1

Library of Congress Cataloging-in-Publication Data is available

Printed in the United States of America

For Liesa Abrams, my angel of editing. Without her amazing skill, insight and friendship, the Sleeper would have never awakened.

PROLOGUE

AWAY FROM PRYING EYES.

The sleeper awoke knowing that his life was in danger.

There was a man somewhere in the thick, dark jungle who had been hired to kill him.

Springing up from the bed of moss and leaves where he was lying, the sleeper was immediately in tune with his surroundings. The jungle was alive with the cries of birds, the chirps and hum of a variety of insects, the growls of nocturnal predators. But the sleeper was silent as he moved through the thick under-brush.

It was a test, his superiors had told him.

They had given him a file on the man who was somewhere nearby, a professional killer known as the Mensajero de Muerte—Messenger of Death. He had read the file with great interest; the messenger was proficient in all means of killing, from guns to knives, poisons to explosives.

The sleeper came to a steep slope, almost vertical, and used the gnarled roots protruding from the face of the muddy cliff to aid his descent. Once down, he again paused to listen to the cacophony of the nighttime jungle. In the distance he heard the sound of a stream and moved toward it.

A fog had developed close to the ground, and it grew thicker as he traveled closer to the water. Carefully he left the concealment of the tropical forest and approached the water, squatting at its side. The movement of the stream was barely discernable below the veil of fog. He plunged his hand down into the liquid's coolness, bringing it up to wash the sweat and residue of sleep from his eyes.

As he rubbed the grime from his face, the fog pulled back momentarily, and out of the corner of his eye he noticed the partial impression in the soft earth left by the sole of a boot.

Death's messenger had been there already.

The sleeper was starting to rise, every sense tingling, when the figure exploded from concealment behind him.

Correction. Death's messenger was still there. Waiting.

The moonlight glinted fleetingly off a lash of thin wire as it passed over his head. Instinctively the sleeper's hand shot up in front of his throat, stopping the garrote from wrapping around his neck. He grunted in agony as the wire dug into the soft flesh of his hand, stopping only when it hit bone. The pain was excruciating, but the alternative was worse.

He drove his heel back into the knee of his attacker. There was a sharp crack and the messenger grunted, his body listing to one side as the garrote went slack, enough for the sleeper to get out from beneath the wire and spin to face his foe.

The messenger had already recovered, the garrote discarded, a knife appearing in his hand. *There would be no second chance.*

The messenger launched himself at the sleeper and the two of them hurtled backward into the stream. The killer was on the sleeper, the blade of his knife descending toward his throat. He shifted his weight beneath the man's attack. The point of the knife plunged through the water and into the streambed where he had been lying.

The sleeper did not have a weapon. It was part of the plan—part of the test.

The thick, cottonlike clouds slid across the velvet

Ecuadorian sky to reveal a fat moon, its jaundiced light shining down into the jungle below, penetrating the openings in the thick canopy of foliage. And as the concealing darkness momentarily burned away, the combatants saw each other for the first time.

Truly saw each other.

The sleeper looked up into the chiseled features of the man who was trying to kill him. He did not look the part at all. This wasn't some wild-eyed lunatic starving for the taste of blood but a professional. He could have been a carpenter or a grocery store manager, but instead he had chosen to make killing his job.

That was where he and his attacker greatly differed.

He had never been given a choice. Killing was all the sleeper had ever known.

And as he saw his attacker, his attacker saw him.

"You're just a ch—" the messenger began in Spanish, but didn't get the chance to finish.

The sleeper's fingers probed the muddy riverbed, wrapping around a jagged rock. He brought his arm up out of the water; rock clutched in his hand, and savagely struck it against the man's temple.

The messenger let out a howl of pain, falling to one side in the stream.

Rock still in hand, the sleeper splashed to his feet, advancing toward his attacker. A deep gash ran from the man's temple to his eyebrows. Blood flowed freely from the open wound. The messenger had managed to retain his knife and held it before himself defensively as he struggled to stand.

Taking aim at the messenger's hand, the sleeper let his rock fly, the crushing impact forcing the killer to drop his weapon.

And then time seemed to slow. The sleeper watched as the rock rolled into the thick foliage and the knife dropped from the killer's grasp into the water.

The messenger wiped blood from his eye with the back of his injured hand while reaching for a weapon holstered beneath his arm with the other.

The sleeper reached down for the knife. His hand closed around the hilt, and he noted that it was still warm from its owner's grip as he plucked it from the stream.

The gun—a nine-millimeter Ruger—had left the leather holster and was swinging in the sleeper's direction.

The sleeper stared into the deep black hole of the muzzle. Calculating the seconds it would take for the killer to aim, for the signal to travel from his brain to the finger now poised on the trigger.

Just enough time for him to strike first.

The sleeper plunged the eight-inch blade into his

attacker's heart as he dove to the left. The pistol fired repeatedly at where he had been standing a second ago.

The messenger tried to remain standing, but the effort was too much, and he dropped to his knees. He was dying.

The sleeper moved closer, gazing into the eyes of the man as his life force left him. He had expected more from this adversary, this professional killer.

The messenger slumped sideways to the ground, a wheezing sound escaping his lungs as he struggled to hold on to his last breath.

Squatting beside the dying man, the sleeper reached down to the assassin's belt, removing a small communication device from its leather case.

"This is Sleeper One," he said casually into the device. "Exercise complete."

There was a brief period of silence, then, "Very good, sleeper one," came the reply. "Proceed to the extraction zone."

The sleeper let the walkie-talkie slip from his grasp. Remembering his injury, he inspected the wound on the side of his hand made by the garrote. He'd need to see a doctor on his return to the base.

He hoped this would be the last test; he was growing tired of these exercises. After all, killing had become second nature to him.

So natural, he could do it in his sleep.

HAWTHORNE, MA
JUNE 8, 2005

At first there is nothing.

Silent black oblivion enfolding body and soul—and then, an instantaneous spark of awareness.

It's like suddenly coming into being in the deepest part of the ocean—so far down that not even the sun burning in the sky can pierce the impenetrable blackness. And as your sense of self grows, you emerge from the bottomless pocket of black, daring to rise, swimming up through the sea of ebony pitch. Ascending.

Awakening.

Tom Lovett opened his eyes, focusing on the white ceiling above his bed. He immediately began to search out the imperfections—the cracks in the plaster and blistering paint that had become familiar and, in a way, comforting since his family had moved to this house. They had lived in Hawthorne, a tiny town northwest of Boston, for just over a year now.

He pulled his arms out from beneath the covers and stretched them over his head, grunted with exertion, and then let them fall limply to his sides. He wasn't especially stiff—a good sign.

He flipped onto his side, reaching for his glasses and watch on the nightstand next to his bed. He put the glasses on and felt his heartbeat quicken, followed by an anticipatory tingling in his scalp, before looking at the time—and, more specifically, the date. He always hated this part.

It had been Tuesday, June 7, when he'd gone to his room to surf the Net before finally giving in to exhaustion. He distinctly remembered shutting down his computer and placing it on the floor beside his bed. Then he'd taken off his glasses and watch before turning out the light and crawling beneath the covers.

Just like any normal person does.

Tom gazed over the side of the bed to see that his computer was there, just as he remembered, but he was still hesitant to look at his watch—to see how much time had passed while he slept.

Disgusted with his lack of courage, Tom resolutely turned onto his back, held the watch up, and focused on its face.

He breathed a sigh of relief.

It was a quarter past seven on Wednesday, June 8.

"Yes," he whispered, slipping the cold metal band around his wrist and snapping the clasp. He pulled back the blankets and sat upright, throwing his bare feet over the side of the bed. Yellow sunlight sneaked into the room from beneath the drawn window shade. It looked like a nice day, in more ways than one.

It was close to two weeks now since he'd last had an attack, Tom thought, glancing at the *Sports Illustrated* swimsuit edition calendar hanging on the wall above his desk. He had marked the last time with a big red *X*. Cautiously he counted the days to be sure. *Yep, thirteen this morning.*

He shuffled across his room toward the door, feeling healthier than he had in months. *It's going to be a good day,* he decided, reaching for the knob, already making plans for that morning and afternoon.

He stumbled slightly as a sudden knock on the door interrupted his thoughts. The door opened, and his mother stuck her head inside the room.

"Oh, you're up," she said, surprised to see him standing there. "Good," she continued, not missing a beat. "Remember you have an appointment with Dr. Powell at eight-thirty, so you might want to get moving if you're planning to shower and have something to eat before we go."

Then, just as suddenly as she'd been there, she was gone, message delivered.

An appointment with Dr. Powell. Tom's stomach did a sudden flip, as if the floor had just dropped from beneath him.

So much for a good day.

She had been awake for a little while, listening to the sounds of a house not her own. The faint hum of the air conditioner in the window, the barely discernible morning radio voices filtering up from the kitchen, the clatter of dishes.

Madison Fitzgerald pushed her face deeper into the pillow and pulled the covers up tighter, trying with no real success to drift back to sleep.

She attempted to ignore the sounds her aunt and uncle were making from the kitchen as they got ready for work. The heavy aroma of coffee enticed her, but she would wait until they were gone.

Until she was alone.

It wasn't like she didn't love her aunt and uncle. Ellen and Marty Arsenault would do anything for family, and letting her stay in their home was a prime example of their enormous generosity.

Madison's parents were in the midst of a divorce, a breakup that seemed to become nastier with each passing day. Mom and Dad had thought it would be best for her to be removed from the war zone until things became more settled. *It's nice of them to think of me. Yeah, right.* But no matter how welcome Ellen and Marty tried to make her feel, it still wasn't *her* home. She wondered if anyplace would ever feel like home again.

Madison listened for the inevitable closing of the back door and the distant sound of a car starting in the garage outside. They wouldn't be back until at least six o'clock that night. Madison wondered what she would do with herself until then.

It had been pretty much the same thing, day in and day out, since she had arrived in Hawthorne almost two weeks ago. She would get up when she couldn't stand to lie there another minute, make her way downstairs for a cup of coffee and maybe a bowl of cereal, and then she would sit, thinking about how blind she had been not to see what was happening to her parents.

The breakup had taken her completely by surprise. At first she thought her mother was joking when she had picked her up from school that cold and rainy March afternoon. *Doesn't it figure it was cold and rainy?*

But the strange, dull look she had seen in her mother's eyes had convinced her otherwise.

Your father and I have decided to split, Mom had said with very little emotion before pulling away from the front of the school. Said so casually, as if she had no idea what a shock this was to her daughter.

Madison rolled onto her side. She wanted to go back to sleep in the worst way, but the dark thoughts had already started to fly around inside her head.

How could I have been so oblivious? she thought. It was all one big lie; her life had been disintegrating and she had been too stupid to notice.

Sometimes she thought that maybe it was a cosmic punishment. Several of her friends' parents had broken up over the years, and she could remember talking with them, proudly bragging that her parents would never split up. She had seriously begun to wonder if this wasn't some higher power's way of sticking it to her.

Closing her eyes tightly, Madison tried to think of nothing, to find that dark, quiet place where she could hide—where she could lose herself in the embrace of unconsciousness, if only for a few more hours.

Chasing sleep.

His mother had the oldies station playing on the car radio again and Tom was tempted to reach out and switch the channel to something less annoying. It wasn't the music; it was the absolutely obnoxious morning show DJs. They thought they were funny but weren't even close. Normally he couldn't stand to listen to them, but this morning he decided to let them stay because he didn't want to get his mother started.

There were other things he wanted to discuss, things that weren't going to make her very happy.

Billy Joel was singing about the faces of a stranger and how we'd love to try them on, *whatever the hell that meant,* as his mother sang along. She didn't know all the words, but that didn't keep her from trying.

They were stopped at a light and Tom glanced through the passenger window at a group of kids his age on the way to school, backpacks slung over their shoulders. The two guys kept shoving each other and play fighting, acting like idiots in an obvious attempt to impress the two girls walking behind them. The girls stuck together, pretending to ignore the guys, but it was apparent that they loved the attention.

What Tom would have given to be a third idiot out on the street.

The light changed to green and they were driving again, the high school kids growing smaller in the side mirror.

"Won't be long before they're finished for another year," his mother commented.

"What?" Tom asked.

"The kids back there," she answered, her eyes going to her rearview mirror. "Probably another week or so and they'll be done for the summer."

Tom played with the excess material at the end of his seat belt. "So that means I'll be done too," he said, no longer looking at his mother. He already knew what she would say. She took the whole homeschooling thing pretty seriously.

She was silent for a minute. "Doesn't work that way for you, my boy. Sorry," she finally said, quickly looking in his direction and then back to the road. "But let's see what we can do about getting you some time off for good behavior. How does that sound?"

It was his turn to be silent.

"How are you doing with your reading? I know you're a little behind on *Grapes of Wrath*, but—"

"I'm fine with it," Tom interrupted.

"What? Fine with being behind or . . . ?"

"No, I'm caught up. I read it over the weekend. I'm working on the essay questions now."

She nodded her approval, pausing at a stop sign before continuing. "Excellent. How are we doing on the math? If you're still having problems with the trigonometry, you'll have to ask your father. That stuff makes my eyes cross."

The DJs were jabbering, laughing raucously at their own jokes, and Tom reached over to turn the volume down. He had something to say and didn't need the competition. He'd been thinking about this moment for some time—thirteen days, to be precise—but hadn't been sure when the time would be right. This looked to be as good a time as any.

"I remember my old trig teacher," his mother was continuing. "Mr. Cunningham. No matter how hard he tried, he just couldn't get it into my thick skull."

"I don't want to be homeschooled anymore," Tom blurted.

His mother acted like she hadn't heard him, gunning the engine of the Toyota Corolla and switching lanes to get around a minivan.

Tom was considering repeating his bombshell when his mother finally responded.

"All right, what brought this on?" she asked, her tone slipping into rational parent mode.

But he was ready. "I haven't had an attack in two weeks," he explained. "I think I might be growing out of it or something. I feel better than I have in ages, and I want to start living like a normal sixteen-year-old."

His mother rapidly tapped the steering wheel with a fingernail, her eyes staring at the road ahead. She was silent, but Tom could practically hear the gears turning in her head as she tried to come up with all the reasons why this wasn't going to work.

"Do you really think that would be smart?" she finally asked, taking her attention away from the road to gaze at him.

It was exactly as he had expected, and he felt himself growing angry. His parents never wanted to hear how he felt about his situation, and normally he would have let them have their way, but not this time. Tom was sure that this time, his condition was changing. *It had to be; it'd been thirteen days.*

Mom removed her right hand from the steering wheel and reached over to gently massage his shoulder. "I think it's great that you're feeling better and that you haven't had an attack in a while, but I'm afraid you're getting your hopes up for nothing. This isn't a condition that just goes away. Once you have it, you have it for the rest of your life, and that's just something we're all going to have to learn to live with."

Tom leaned toward his door so that his mother's comforting hand would fall away. "It's different this time," he responded.

She sighed, returning her hand to the wheel. Tom noticed that her knuckles had gone white, she was gripping it so tightly. "I hate to be a doomsayer, but you've gone two weeks without an attack before—and then had one. What makes you think this time is any different?"

Tom looked out the window at the cars zipping past him in the right-hand lane. "I stopped taking my medication," he said in a voice far softer than he had intended. If she didn't blow up at this, he figured he was doing all right.

"You what!" his mother yelled, and the car swerved slightly to the left as if she had momentarily lost control.

So much for me doing all right, Tom thought.

"Tell me you're joking," she demanded. Her cheeks were flushed red, and she had the wild look in her eyes that she got when she was about to lose it. It was the same look she'd gotten a few months back when he had ridden his bike to Butler, the decommissioned air force base about twenty miles from his house.

"Do you realize how dangerous that is?" she yelled. "How could you do something so stupid without telling your father and me?"

"I'm fine," he yelled back. "I haven't taken any medicine in over a week and I feel fine. Shouldn't that tell you something?"

They were coming up on their exit and he was getting ready to point it out, but it wasn't necessary. His mother threw on her blinker and swerved into the right lane, cutting off a delivery truck.

"It tells me that you're not thinking," she said, clicking on the blinker again for the exit. "It tells me that you're so desperate not to have your condition that you'd be willing to believe just about anything."

She took the exit a little too sharply, the car's tires screeching shrilly as he was pushed against the door by the momentum of the turn.

"That's not true," he shot back. "I gave it a lot of thought before I did it. If I'd had an attack, I would have started taking the medicine again, but I haven't." He scowled at her from his seat. "I'm not stupid, you know."

"I'm so angry at you right now I'm not so sure," his mother said through gritted teeth, obviously trying to remain calm.

"You're just being overprotective," Tom said defensively. "I'm fine—I really am."

She turned right onto York Street and then left into the Monarch Plaza parking lot, where Dr. Powell had his office.

"We'll see what the doctor says about that," she said, pulling into a space and throwing the car into park. She threw her car keys into her bag, opened the door, and slammed it shut behind her.

Tom leaned his head back against the seat and sighed. All things considered, it had gone better than he expected.

Narcolepsy is a potentially disabling, lifelong neurological condition estimated to afflict about one in every two thousand people in the United States. The disorder is best characterized as an inability of the nervous system to maintain the boundaries between wakefulness and sleep. During usual waking hours, people experience periods when sleep involuntarily encroaches into wakefulness. Those stricken with the quite rare and severely incapacitating version of the sleep disorder, Quentin's narcolepsy, can experience periods of perpetual sleep that in some cases have lasted anywhere from a single day to five days.

Dr. Bernard Quentin
From the article "A New Narcolepsy"
Published by the International Research
Foundation for Sleep Disorders (IRFSD), 1982

"Deep breath," Dr. Powell ordered, and Tom did as he was told. The stethoscope was cold against his bare chest, as it always seemed to be.

Powell was short, with a beard, a little on the heavy side, and his breath always smelled like peppermint. Tom liked him; he seemed to be a good guy, not a stiff like some of the other doctors he had seen over the years. Dr. Powell had been Tom's physician since his father's most recent assignment had brought the family to Hawthorne a year ago. Dad's job as a mathematical troubleshooter for high-technology firms forced them to relocate a lot; Dr. Powell was the fourth specialist Tom had seen since he was eight years old and first diagnosed with Quentin's narcolepsy.

"Good," the doctor said. He stepped away from the exam table, placing the stethoscope around his neck. "You can put your shirt back on," he said over his shoulder as he grabbed a manila file folder. He plucked a pen from his white lab coat pocket and began to jot down a few notes.

"So," Powell said, still writing. "Anything you'd like to tell me about? Anything you think I should know?"

Tom's mother had gotten to Powell first, having a little closed-door one-on-one with the doctor before Tom was called in for his examination. He'd known it was only a matter of time before the doctor brought it up.

Tom shrugged, his feet dangling off exam table where he still sat. "I stopped taking my meds," he said quietly.

Dr. Powell looked up. "You stopped taking your meds?" he repeated sharply, then began to leaf through the medical file. "I don't see anywhere in my notes here that I told you to do that." The doctor closed the folder and fixed the Tom with a stare so intense he could practically feel it. "Help me out here, Tom. When did I tell you to do this?"

Tom studied a hangnail on his thumb, but he could still feel the man's eyes boring into him. "You didn't," he mumbled, glancing up nervously.

"I didn't," Dr. Powell echoed with a slow nod. He set the file down on the countertop and placed his pen back inside his coat pocket. "That's a relief," he said, pretending to wipe beads of sweat from his brow. "Because I sure as hell don't remember encouraging you to do anything that stupid."

Tom laughed nervously. "I'm sorry. It's just that I was feeling better, so I decided to experiment. Where's the harm in—?"

"Where's the harm?" Powell interrupted. "Tom, Quentin's narcolepsy is a disorder that we still know very little about. The medications we put you on are to help you manage the disorder so that you can lead as normal a life as possible. When you stop taking them, your blood levels—"

"Normal life?" It was Tom's turn to interrupt, his voice rising an octave. "I don't lead a normal life." He felt the anger growing again. Sure, it could have been worse: he could have been in a wheelchair or have some kind of cancer, but it was still bad. He felt like he was living in a bubble, looking out at a much bigger world. He took a deep breath.

"I feel fine," he said more calmly. "I haven't had an attack in thirteen days and I've been without medications for a week."

Powell approached the examination table and put a supportive hand on his shoulder. "You feel fine now, but what about next week or a month from now when the spells hit you again?" he asked quietly. "Quentin's narcolepsy does not go away, Tom. It's not something you outgrow. It's a genetic disorder."

"But you yourself said that there's lots still unknown about the disease," Tom argued. "Maybe there's a chance that the symptoms do decrease with age."

Dr. Powell gently squeezed the tensed muscles in his shoulder. "We have enough information about normal narcolepsy to know that it's a lifelong ailment that requires medications and lifestyle modifications to control its symptoms."

"But I feel fine," Tom whispered, hanging his head low.

"And I think it's wonderful that you're feeling so good," Dr. Powell said, picking up the file again. "But I'm sorry, Tom, that doesn't mean you're free of the sickness. In fact, I'd be even more vigilant with medicines and routines now that you're starting to see this level of success so you don't throw off the stability you've worked so hard to achieve."

Powell walked to the examination room door and rested his hand on the knob. "Your mother's very concerned, you know."

Tom laughed sarcastically. "When isn't she?"

"Your parents just want what's best for you," the doctor replied. "I'm sure they can be a little overprotective, but it's only because they care." He motioned with the manila folder for Tom to follow. "Come on into my office and we can talk this through with your mom."

Tom slid off the table and followed Dr. Powell into his office, where Victoria Lovett was waiting for them. She had been on the phone and was quickly putting the cell back into her purse. *Probably on the phone with Dad,* he thought. *Busted.*

She still didn't look happy.

"Well?" she asked from her seat in front of Dr. Powell's desk. "Is he all right?"

Powell sat down at his desk. "He's fine as far as I can see," he answered, arranging some paperwork in front of him. "I'd like to take some blood before he leaves, just to be sure."

Tom sat down in the empty chair next to his mother, doing everything he could not to make eye contact with her.

"I can't believe he did this," she continued. "After we worked so hard to cut down on the attacks, this is what he does."

"I'm sorry," Tom said again, his anger returning. "I get it; you're upset. I'll start taking the medication again when I get home, so just calm down."

"Calm down?" his mother yelled, shifting in her seat so she could address him directly. "Don't you think I have reason to be upset?" she asked. "My only child has stopped taking the medicine that keeps him from falling asleep for days at a time and he doesn't understand why I'm upset?"

He hadn't thought that it would be this big a deal. Part of him had hoped that his mother would be psyched that he was feeling so much better. The thing was, the more he thought about it, as much as it burned him to admit it, he was starting to see her point. He didn't say anything, staring at the office floor, at the swirling red pattern in the rug beneath his feet. Tom didn't want to be there anymore; he wanted to go home—to his bubble.

"We could change some of his medications, maybe up the antidepressant a bit, but I'd like to look at his blood work first," Dr. Powell interjected.

Images of pills danced in Tom's head: tiny white pills, black-and-orange time-released caplets, ones that resembled Skittles candies. Dexedrine, Provigil, Tofranil, Norpramin, Anafranil, Cylert.

From far away, he heard his mother and Dr. Powell discuss his medicine, and then the doctor picked up the phone and dialed the lab. He listened to Dr. Powell speak. It was as if the doc were speaking from inside a public restroom. Something was wrong.

Not this, Tom thought, *please, not now*. He started to stand.

"We can't go until Dr. Powell takes some blood," his mother was explaining. "Tom, are you all right?" she asked, and though she sounded far away, Tom could detect the concern in her voice.

"Gotta go," he managed, sounding like he was speaking in slow motion. His limbs felt heavy, as if they had been filled with lead.

"Tom?" he barely heard Dr. Powell say, and there was a commotion and a brief flash of pain and he realized that he had fallen to the floor.

They were right. The world turned black and began to

close in all around him. He wasn't better. It had been wait-ing for him all along. Patiently waiting until he let his guard down, letting him think that he might have a chance.

What a jerk he'd been.

He would never be normal.

Never.

After eight years with Quentin's narcolepsy, Tom should have been used to the attacks. *Oh, well, here comes another one, better aim for something soft.*

But that wasn't the case.

They came on him with very little warning. Sometimes he would find himself suddenly emotional, very excited about nothing in particular or really pissed off. That was usually a good indicator, but by the time he realized it, it was often way too late. The loss of muscle control was next. Medically it was called a cataleptic attack. He would get very weak, his arms and legs feeling like they were made out of rubber—or like they suddenly weighed a thousand pounds each. Yeah, this was the fun stuff, the warm-up to a full-on narcoleptic episode. And as if things weren't exciting enough, there were the hallucinations. He'd been having more of those lately, but not this time.

He could think of nothing worse than what he was experiencing on the floor of his doctor's office, that feeling of helplessness as the darkness opened wide to swallow him. Tom could hear his mother's voice, far, far away, telling him that he was fine, encouraging him to ride it out, and he knew that she was right. But there was still that nagging question in the back of his mind: *What if this is it?* What if he was dragged so deep into the darkness that he never woke up?

It could happen. There was so much they didn't understand about the illness.

He'd been out for five full days once. *Five days.*

Want to make it six? Tom imagined the darkness asking as it pulled him deeper. *Come on down, we have plenty of room. Stay as long as you like.*

His body reacted, thrashing wildly, the side of his face bouncing off the carpeted floor, followed by a sudden surge of adrenaline that allowed him to escape the clutches of sleep, but only for a brief instant before he was lost again. It was too strong. No matter how hard he fought, the spell would beat him; it was a horrible lesson that he had learned over the years and one that he would have to accept all over again now that he knew the affliction had not left him.

The worst part of an attack was when the darkness of sleep took him whole. It dragged him so deep that all sense of self disappeared, and at that moment he didn't seem to exist anymore.

Tom imagined that it was an awful lot like dying.

3

CHAPTER

Madison shuffled into the kitchen, her slippers sliding on the tile floor as she crossed to the cabinet to get herself a cup for her morning coffee. She poured herself a full mug and then splashed some milk in, watching the color change from nearly black to a light brown before taking a sip.

She made her way to the island in the center of the kitchen and grabbed a banana from the fruit bowl. DJs jabbered softly from a radio, but Madison wasn't hearing them. Already she found herself lost inside her head, thinking about her parents.

If only they had told me sooner, she thought, taking another swig of coffee.

"I have to get a life," Madison muttered.

She finished her banana and pushed her stool away from the island, bringing the peel to the trash. She caught a snippet of a Rolling Stones song playing on the radio. Her dad loved Mick Jagger, and she had to laugh, remembering the really horrible imitation he did whenever a Stones song came on back home.

A wave of sadness washed over her, and Madison found herself reaching for the cordless phone attached to the wall, checking the time showing on the microwave as she dialed a number she knew by heart. He should be in his office now, she thought, pacing in a circle, listening to the sound of the phone's ring.

"Steven Fitzgerald, how can I help you?" answered a voice.

Madison smiled. "Hey, Dad," she said. "It's me."

"Hey, me, how's it going?"

She went back to her stool and sat down. "Okay," she said. "Aunt Ellen and Uncle Marty haven't thrown me out yet, so it can't be going too badly."

Her father laughed, and she wondered how often he actually did that these days. "Hold on for a second, would ya, hon?" he asked, and the sound on the other end of the phone muffled as he placed his hand over the mouthpiece and began to talk with someone. Her father worked at the registrar's office at the University of Chicago.

"Sorry about that, kiddo," her dad said, coming back to her.

"That's all right. You busy?"

"No more than usual," he replied. "What've you been up to? Pahking your cah in Havahd Yahd?" he asked in a horrible attempt at a New England accent.

Madison started to giggle. It was cool to hear him joking for the first time in . . . a while.

"People do *not* talk like that around here," she said with a laugh.

"Yeah, right," he said in mock disgust. "Next time I see you, I won't be able to understand a word you're saying."

They shared another laugh and as it died down, Madison ventured, "Talk to Mom lately?"

There was quiet on the other end of the phone.

"Dad?" she prodded. "Have you talked to . . . ?"

"I heard you the first time," her father answered. There was no longer any hint of humor in his voice. "No. No, I haven't. Your mother and I . . . Your mother and I don't . . . Well, it's not that we don't, we just can't talk nicely to each other anymore."

Madison felt a tightness come into her throat. "What do you mean you can't talk to each other? Of course you can talk to each other. You just pick up the phone and call the house."

Her father sighed heavily into the receiver. "Madison, please," he begged her. "Your mother and I are going through some pretty rough stuff right now, and it's just hard to be civil with each other."

She did not want to hear this. She wanted to hear that her father and mother had been talking, that they were working things out.

"And our lawyers have recommended that we shouldn't—"

"I don't want to hear about your damn lawyers," Madison yelled into the phone, slamming her hand down on the island.

"Madison, please," her father pleaded again. "How many times do we have to have this conversation?" She could hear the annoyance in his voice.

"I guess until I really understand what happened between you and Mom," she said curtly.

An uncomfortable silence expanded between them, and for a moment she began to wonder if her father was even there anymore.

"There's really not all that much to understand," he finally said, his voice startling after the quiet. "We drifted apart. And by the time we noticed, we'd gone too far, become different people."

Madison slid off the stool and began to pace around the kitchen, phone pressed tightly to her ear. "That's not true. You were happy. I would have known if something was wrong."

"I'm not going to say it was all bad, but you saw

what we wanted you to see, honey," her father tried to explain, his voice sad. "We became good at hiding it from you. We didn't want you to know until we thought you'd be able to handle it."

She had started to cry, tears running down her face. "Well, you know what?" she asked, wiping her running nose with the back of her hand. "I wasn't ready, and I'm not sure if I would've ever been ready to learn that my parents were living a lie." She grabbed a tissue from the box on the counter and wiped her tears. "It's like some crazy bad dream that keeps tricking me into thinking that I'm awake, but I'm really not, and it just keeps going on and on."

She heard her father breathing on the other end of the line. "I know this is tough for you, honey," he said. "But it's tough for us as well."

Madison laughed. "Yeah, right, especially all that fighting your lawyers are doing over who gets the house and who gets the car, right?"

It was usually at this point that her father lost control, going off about how he wished his daughter would cut him some slack. But today was different.

"I really have to go," he said, the tight control obvious in his tone.

"Yeah." She sniffed. "I've got to get going too."

"Madison, I—" her father started.

"Talk to you later," she cut in, not allowing him to finish.

"All right," her father responded. "Talk to you soon."

Madison slammed the phone back into its cradle, certain that he was going to say that he loved her or something equally infuriating. She snatched up her coffee, taking a big gulp, grimacing as the cold, bitter liquid traveled down her throat.

She dumped what was left into the sink.

She thought about what her father had said. Digging through her memories—school plays, First Holy Communion, Christmases down the line—she searched the past for hidden problems, for evidence of lies. She couldn't come up with any.

But that doesn't mean they weren't there.

It had been a morning filled with so much potential, and Tom was amazed by how quickly it had all turned into a steaming pile of crap.

He had awakened on the table in Dr. Powell's exam room, both the doctor and his mom standing close by, waiting for the spell to run its course. He'd been asleep for over an hour.

Would have served them right if I was out for a week, he thought angrily, not really sure why he was so mad at them but guessing it had something to do with the fact that they had ended up being right. He wasn't getting any better; in fact, he was the same as he'd always been. Tom's hand drifted up to gently touch the nasty bump on his forehead. It hurt like hell, and he had the beginnings of a major headache.

"Are you okay?" his mother asked from the driving seat. He ignored her question, staring out the window but really seeing nothing.

"I knew you'd hurt yourself," she said. "The way you were thrashing around. This is why I was so upset that you weren't taking your—"

"Could we please not talk about this?" he begged her. "Please?"

His mother turned in at their driveway on Burrows Place, a quiet cul-de-sac that they shared with one other home. Tom was surprised to see that they were home already. He had been so lost in his angry thoughts that he had barely registered the ride from the doctor's office.

"Do you want me to make you some lunch?" Mom asked, glancing at her watch. "It's nearly quarter to twelve."

"I'm not hungry," Tom grumbled, opening the car door and getting out. But he had forgotten his keys, so he had to wait at the front door for his mother to let him inside.

"See, you need me for something," she said with a smirk, opening the door and holding it for him to enter. "How about I make us a couple of grilled cheese sandwiches? I have some pickles, and I think there might be some chips left—if your father hasn't eaten them all."

"I'll pass," Tom said, heading through the living room on his way to the kitchen.

"Well, you have to eat something," she said as she followed him.

Tom went to the fridge and poured himself a glass of orange juice.

His mother leaned against the stove, watching as he put down his glass and went to the cabinet where he kept his medications—out of sight, but always waiting.

"I'll probably be too full to eat anything anyway once I finish taking all these," he snarled, pulling multiple pill bottles down from the shelf. He carried them over to where he'd left his juice and let them spill from his arms onto the counter. "Hmmm," he said, placing a finger on his chin as if deep in thought. "Which one should I take first?" He smacked his lips as if ready to sit down to a delicious meal.

"Stop it, Tom." His mother pushed off the stove to come and stand by his side. "You have to know that this is for your own good—you saw what happened today."

"I think I'll start with the Cylert," Tom continued,

ignoring her and snatching the bottle up from the counter. He popped the pill into his mouth, washing it down with a big gulp of juice.

"Delicious." He picked up another bottle. "I think I'll go with the antidepressant next, 'cause I'm feeling a bit out of sorts since being reminded that my life is crap." He pulled off the bottle top and was about to shake out a capsule when his mother grabbed hold of his hand.

"Please stop," she begged him. "I can't stand to see you act like this."

"And how do you think I should be acting, Mom?" he asked. "Should I just shrug, say, 'Oh, well, sucks for me,' and slip back into the old routine?" He pulled his hand away from her. "I hate the old routine." He took a capsule from the bottle he was holding and placed it in his mouth. "I hate it."

His mother ran her hands through her shoulder-length blond hair and leaned against the counter. "Look, when you were first diagnosed with Quentin's narcolepsy, we made a promise, your dad and I, that you weren't going to go through this alone."

Tom picked up his glass and took a drink, washing down the next pill as he half listened. He drifted back to his first attack, how scared they had all been. They'd been living in Sweetwater, Texas, then, and it had been his first day of third grade at East Ridge Elementary School. Initially they had blamed it on the heat, but then it kept happening, and soon he became known as the strange little kid who couldn't keep from falling asleep.

He didn't go to East Ridge for very long.

"We said we would be here every step of the way for you," his mother's voice droned. How many times had he heard this speech? "In times when things seem to be going all right and times very much like this, when things aren't so good." She smiled at him then, a warm, loving smile—a mother's smile. "We'll always be here for you. I hope you can believe that."

She only succeeded in making him feel worse. He saw himself as an old man—thirty-five, maybe forty years old, still living with his parents, still following the same routines. He heard their voices, gravelly with age, asking him if he'd taken his pills.

"Tom?" His mother's voice shook him from the nightmarish scenario. "Did you hear what I said?"

"Yeah, I heard." He nodded. "And I appreciate it." He tried to sound grateful.

Mom folded her arms across her chest and sighed. "What's wrong now?" she prodded. "Did I say something else to upset you?"

"I don't mean to make you feel bad," he started to explain, glancing over at his mother, "but I don't want you and Dad around me forever. I don't want to have to be dependent on somebody else my entire life."

His mother didn't respond, so Tom continued. "I want a life of my own. I want to finish school, go to college, get a degree and a really good job making some serious money."

His mother was smiling now.

"What, no girls?" she asked. "Not going to meet anybody special in college? Get married? Have a dozen kids?"

Tom almost continued, but reality came crashing in all around him and he found himself even more depressed than before. "Why are we even talking about this?" he snapped. "You know as well as I do that there won't be any college, that any job I get will probably be something set up by the state for people with disabilities, and as far as girls go, I don't think they'd be very interested in a guy who can't stay awake on a date."

"Tom, don't do this to yourself," she said. "Dr. Powell said that they're learning more about Quentin's all the time. There's always a chance that they'll develop a new medication that will allow you to be like everybody else."

He laughed sadly, shaking his head. "And there's the problem. Most of the time I already *feel* like everybody else, but deep down I know I'm not—I *never* will be, and that's what makes me so freaking angry."

Madison wasn't sure if she had read it in one of the books on children and divorce that her mother had bought for her or if maybe she'd seen it on *Dr. Phil*. The best way to deal when your life was in turmoil—to return to some sense of normalcy—was to develop positive routines, things done on a daily basis at specific times.

She slid the glass door aside and stepped out onto the back deck. Sleeping late and having daily screaming matches on the phone with her parents probably wouldn't be considered positive.

Still, she had managed to pull herself together relatively early today. Showering and getting clothes on before one in the afternoon was a pretty big achievement for her these days, so maybe this was the beginning of a return to normalcy.

Madison brushed off a chair and sat down. She slouched, stretching her long legs out in front of her. The pink polish on her toenails had started to chip, and she made a mental note to put a fresh coat on them sometime today. It was all about establishing positive routines, right?

She gazed cautiously at the journal resting in her

lap. She hadn't touched it since coming to Hawthorne, hadn't even had the urge.

And Madison loved to write. She'd always kept a journal and had written articles for her junior high and high school newspapers. In fact, last year, her sophomore year, she'd been a finalist for the Hemingway Writing Awards for High School Journalists. She hadn't won, but being nominated had been pretty cool.

Today she would get back into her writing. Taking a deep breath, she opened the leather cover to her journal and began to slowly leaf through the pages where she had written her thoughts. She stopped to read snippets here and there, trying to relive those past moments. It was the pages about her old boyfriend that finally did it. Zack had broken up with her two months before the sophomore prom, and even though it was a year ago, it still stung.

She scanned the entries. At that point, life as she knew it had been coming to an end. Madison smiled as she flipped through the journal. She'd shown him. She *had* gone without him and had a great time.

So shouldn't that give her hope that she could survive her parents' breakup now? *What's that thing people always say when they're trying to make you feel better?* "*Time heals all wounds.*" It annoyed her to admit it, but there could be some truth to the words.

She turned the pages until she found a clean one and scribbled the date at the top of the page. *Purge yourself of your emotions,* she told herself. At first it was difficult, and she was tempted to stop, to go into the house and turn on the television, but Madison stuck with it. She started slowly but gathered speed as more and more of her thoughts started to come together. It was painful but gratifying.

She wasn't sure how long she'd been writing, but suddenly she realized that her wrist was sore, and she had filled nearly twelve pages with her crazy handwriting. She put the cover back on her pen and closed the journal with a deep sigh. It wasn't exactly a cure for the pain, but it certainly helped her to put things in perspective. And it did actually feel good to be doing something constructive again.

The first of my new positive routines, she considered, standing up and stretching her arms above her head.

The gas grill at the end of the back deck caught her eye, and she had the idea to make dinner for her aunt and uncle that night. *Wouldn't that blow their minds,* she thought. *Nothing fancy, just some burgers.*

Madison was about to head inside to see if they had what she would need when she saw movement in the yard across the way. She had been living here for almost two weeks but had never seen a soul from the house next door. She knew that somebody lived there, of course: there were cars in the driveway that came and went, lights on and off, but she had never been able to catch sight of the only neighbors on their little block.

Curiosity got the better of her, and she casually strolled to the end of the deck, craning her neck to look over the strategically placed bushes and the wooden fence behind them.

She was surprised to see a guy around her age, tall-ish, with short, sandy blond hair and glasses, playing basketball by himself. She took a few steps closer, checking him out. He was wearing jeans and a short-sleeve T-shirt, and even from a distance she could tell he was in incredible shape.

I might just find another positive routine around here, she thought.

Tom had been playing basketball for an hour and knew he should be resting, but he just didn't want to deal. Living with the constant threat of falling asleep made taking naps seem so unnecessary, no matter what Dr. Powell and the National Sleep Foundation said.

Instead he went down to the basement family room, grabbing his books and notebook along the way. He decided to work on the essay questions for *The Grapes of Wrath*. He sat down at the desk and flipped on the power strip with his foot. The computer hummed to life while he thumbed through his notebook, searching for the notes he'd already written on the first few questions.

"All right," he said, shifting in the office chair and turning his attention to the computer. He opened a folder labeled Tom's Schoolwork and then the file dedicated to his literature essays.

...anced down at the page where he had written ...otes and was preparing to type his opening paragraph when he felt the world drop out from beneath him.

"Whoa," he said aloud as he was hit with a wave of vertigo. He was still looking down at his notebook, but the handwriting had begun to blur, the words to unravel, the ink lines loosening and lifting off the page to drift in the air in front of him.

Please, no.

Tom tried to stay calm. It was a hypnagogic hallucination, another delightful symptom of narcolepsy, and this was looking to be a wild one.

I should've taken that nap, he scolded himself, feeling his heart begin to race, his breathing speed up. He watched as the words from his essay drifted up from the white notebook, slowly unraveling into threads of black, moving like snakes in the air. Tom moved his head so that they wouldn't crash into his face.

He reached out to touch one of the threads, one that he believed had once formed the name Steinbeck, but discovered much to his surprise that he too had become weightless. Tom was drifting up and out of his seat, the black lines of the words he had written hovering around him as he floated up toward the family room ceiling.

This is definitely one of the weirder ones, he thought as the ceiling loomed closer. And he had to wonder if the strength and strangeness of the delusion had anything to do with not taking his medication. Tom made a mental note *not* to mention this to his mother.

The white stucco ceiling was in front of his face, and he prepared for impact, but it didn't come. Instead he floated ghostlike up through the ceiling, then the kitchen on the first floor above, the second floor, and finally out through the roof to hover above his home.

Too freakin' bizarre, he thought. Tom knew he should just relax and ride out the experience, but there was something that didn't feel right, something that made him uneasy.

No matter how hard he tried, he couldn't stop his skyward progress.

He started to tremble; he imagined the cold winds of what at this point had to be the stratosphere sucking the warmth from his body.

His skin had become numb, and he could see a fine sheen of frost forming on the hair of his bare arms. The air was growing thinner, and it was getting harder and harder to breathe.

It's only a matter of time now, he thought, remembering something he had seen on the Discovery Channel about what happens to a body when exposed to the vacuum of space. From movies, most people believe that your body explodes in a vacuum. But that's not what happens.

Tom felt himself begin to convulse, his lungs struggling for oxygen.

It's really a lot like drowning, he imagined.

Drowning among the stars.

Just as suddenly as it started, Tom was free of the hallucination's hold and he tumbled from his chair onto the floor. He lay there gasping for breath, his body twitching with chills.

"Were you having a daymare?" asked a voice from across the room, and Tom realized his father had come downstairs. "Daymare?" Mason asked again, using Tom's childhood name for these waking dreams. "Are you okay?"

Tom nodded. "Yeah. It was a bad one." Embarrassed, he quickly picked himself up and began to gather the school papers that he had knocked off the desk. "How long have you been there?"

"Not long," Mason answered from the leather recliner across the room. He had a bottle of water and removed the cap, taking a sip. "What was it like this time?"

"Just stupid crap," Tom answered. He sat back

down at the computer and tried to look busy, but he could feel the tension in the room and knew that his mother had already shared the fact that he hadn't been taking his medication. "It was another floating one, only this time I went up through the ceiling and kept right on going into space."

Dad nodded, taking another pull from his water bottle. "Sounded like you were having some problems breathing," he explained coolly. Mason Lovett did just about everything coolly. Tom figured it had something to do with his job as a mathematical troubleshooter. It was difficult to read his father, and Tom wasn't sure yet if he was in deep trouble or simply having a normal conversation.

Tom swiveled nervously from side to side in the chair. "Yeah, I couldn't breathe once I got high enough. I even thought I had frost forming on my arms. This one was a trip."

His father nodded again. "Sounds like it," he said. "Do you think the fact that you haven't been taking your medicine had anything to do with how bad this one was?"

Tom shrugged, deciding that the papers on his desk weren't quite straight enough. "I'm sure it had something to do with it." He didn't want to look at his father; there was nothing that freaked him out more than the look Mason Lovett got in his eyes when he was disappointed or angry. Tom and his mother secretly called it the death-ray stare.

"Do you like having these attacks, Tom?" his father asked. "Do you enjoy falling asleep at the drop of a hat, smashing your head on furniture, and having hallucinations that you're floating off into space to suffocate?"

Tom found himself touching his bump and quickly pulled his hand away. The funny thing about Mason Lovett was that even when he was really angry, he never raised his voice. Tom had learned to listen carefully to every word to figure out his father's mood. He understood the meaning of these words very well; he was in serious trouble and braced himself for what was coming.

"I know it was dumb," Tom said, hoping to defuse some of his father's anger. "A really stupid move." He glanced quickly at Mason, who still sat in the leather chair, death-ray eyes blazing.

"Well, at least we can agree on that," his father said. "But what I want to know is how someone as smart as you are could even think that something so obviously stupid was the right thing to do."

Tom knew that it was probably in his best interests to keep his mouth shut, to endure the withering stare until his father got it all out of his system and went back upstairs to help Mom with dinner and watch the nightly news. But he just couldn't do it this time.

"I thought . . . I was feeling really good and—"

"Did you realize the risk you would be taking?" Mason asked. He set his half-empty water bottle down on the rug as he leaned forward in the leather chair. "This is your health we're talking about—your life."

"And I thought that there might be a chance for something more than *my life*, and I grabbed at it. Do you have any idea how it feels to be like this?"

He wanted his father to realize that what he had done wasn't just because he was some stupid kid who didn't understand the seriousness of the situation. He understood very well and had been willing to take the risk just the same.

Mason stood up, his tall figure suddenly looming over Tom at the desk chair. "I know it's hard for you, son," he said. "Believe me, I know, but it doesn't change the facts. You're sick, whether you want to be or not. And the only way you're going to be able to live any semblance of a normal life—a life that your mother and I want for you—is by doing what you're supposed to do."

Tom nodded, defeated.

Madison reached across the kitchen table for the large glass bowl and another helping of salad.

"So, besides making us this fabulous supper, what did you do today?" Ellen asked, picking up her hamburger.

"Nothing much," Madison answered, nibbling a bite of lettuce off her fork. "What do you know about the guy next door?" she asked.

"The boy next door?" Ellen asked. "You know, not a lot. Why, did you see him today?"

Madison took another bite of salad. "He was playing basketball in his yard. I saw him from the deck."

"We don't see him much," her uncle cut in. "We could probably count on one hand the number of times we've seen any of them next door since they moved in—what? A year ago, was it?"

Ellen nodded.

"He's probably about your age, though," Marty said, taking a bite of his burger.

"And cute," her aunt added, making Madison do a double take before letting out a nervous giggle.

She had always been close to Ellen and Marty, but there was still so much about them that she didn't know, like why they had never had children of their own. They seemed like they would have been really good parents.

"What, you think I'm too old to notice?" Ellen nudged Madison. "Admit it, you think he's cute."

Madison blushed, and soon they were both giggling. Madison suddenly remembered what it felt like to joke around, to be happy. "I might just have to climb over that fence tomorrow to get a better look," she answered.

"Think he'd be worth the climb?" Ellen asked.

She felt her cheeks flush with the memory of watching the guy as he played. "Probably." She started to giggle again.

"Maybe he'll be in some of your classes this fall," her uncle happily interjected.

Madison's face fell as Marty's comment sank in. "Why would he be in my classes this fall?" she asked with tightness in her voice, already anticipating the answer.

Marty was desperate, looking to his wife for support. "Whoops," he said with a grimace.

Madison looked from her uncle to her aunt. "What did he mean?" she asked. "Why would he be in my classes?"

Ellen shifted in her seat uncomfortably. "Good one, Marty," she muttered before turning her attention to her niece. "We were going to tell you this later," Ellen said softly, "but seeing as it's already been brought up . . ."

"Discuss what?" Madison's muscles tensed.

"I talked to your mom today, and she feels that it would be best for you to stay here with us rather than go back to Chicago at the end of the summer. She'd like you to attend school here."

Madison leaned back in her chair. She took a deep breath, trying to stay calm, but no amount of breathing was going to diminish the anger rising in her chest. It was her senior year—her last year of high school.

"This is bullshit!" she cried. "Complete bullshit!"

"Madison, please calm down," Marty said. "We know that this is upsetting, but the divorce is going to take a while, and to tell you the truth, things aren't going all that peacefully. . . ."

Madison abruptly stood. The silverware jangled noisily as her hip bumped the table edge, and then the kitchen fell into an uncomfortable silence.

"Why is it that everybody is always making decisions about what's best for me without asking me what *I* think?" Madison stared at her aunt and uncle. They didn't deserve this, but they were the closest thing to parents in the general vicinity.

"Home just isn't the place for you to be right now, honey," Aunt Ellen said, nervously picking up her wineglass and taking a long sip.

Madison thought about everything that she had left behind: her friends, her job, her parents—even though she wanted to kill them both at the moment—and home. She had left before school let out, only on the condition that she would return at the end of the summer. After all, summer was only a few months long, and she knew that a distraction from the fighting might be a good thing.

She could still hear her mother as she packed her things two weeks ago, and suddenly those words took on a whole new meaning.

Don't think of it as a bad thing, she had said. *Think of it as a fresh start.*

"Maddy, sit down," her uncle said, reaching over to pat the seat of her chair. "Let's talk about this."

She moved away from the table, heading for the deck. "I really don't feel like talking right now."

The nighttime air was cool, although the official start of summer was just a couple of weeks away. Madison breathed in the New England night as she closed the door behind her, hoping that her aunt and uncle wouldn't follow her out.

She walked farther onto the back of the deck, standing in the darkness and looking out over the yard. *What am I going to do?* She felt her eyes begin to well with tears. The most frustrating thing was that she couldn't do anything—she didn't have a choice.

From the corner of her eye she saw something move and glanced over to her right, into the neighbors' yard.

It was draped in shadows, but she could just make out the shape of somebody sitting alone. An arm rose in the darkness to swat away a bug, and she realized that it was the guy she had seen earlier. The first thought that flashed through her brain was how strange it was that he was out there in the dark alone. Then she realized—*hello*, so was she.

Kindred spirits.

Tom had made a conscious decision to return to his usual routine.

Sitting in the yard last night, he had thought about his life and what he wanted from it and knew that there was no way his illness could not be factored in. Quentin's narcolepsy was here to stay.

What choice do I have? he had asked himself in the darkness. His decision had been obvious, common sense, really. And although it was easier said than done, he had run out of other options.

"Accept your illness as a part of what makes you you," a psychologist had once said to him. *"Embrace it."* That guy hadn't lasted long. In no way did Tom want to give his narcolepsy a hug, but he did have to learn to live with it.

He hadn't wasted any time getting back into the swing of things. It was a schedule first created by his parents and then tweaked as he had gotten older. He got up around seven, ate breakfast, took his medication, and showered. Schoolwork was his next priority, broken up with periodic exercise, a bike ride, a run around the neighborhood, weight training, martial arts with his dad. Exercise was always followed by a brief nap to recharge his batteries so he didn't get overtired and trigger an attack.

That was his day—how it was supposed to be, and would be, as he realigned his way of thinking.

Now Tom was sitting at the patio table in his backyard, finishing schoolwork. Something flew over his shoulder and hit the screen of his laptop. Tom leapt to his feet, knocking his chair over behind him. His heart hammered in his chest as he stared at the object on the table in front of him.

A Frisbee. A blue Frisbee.

He picked it up and turned around to find a girl climbing over the neighbors' fence. He had never seen her before.

"I am so sorry," she said, her voice muffled slightly by the hand that covered her mouth.

"Scared me," Tom replied with a nervous laugh and an uncomfortable smile. He had no idea who she was, but she was definitely hot. The girl was about his height, with auburn hair pulled back. She had pale, soft-looking skin and wide eyes.

She moved her hand away from her mouth and walked slowly toward him. He noticed she was wearing a T-shirt and white shorts; he tried not to stare at her legs. "You're not mad, are you?" she asked with an embarrassed grin.

Tom shook his head. He couldn't take his eyes off her. "Nah, I'm fine. You just surprised me is all."

"I'm Madison Fitzgerald," she said, sticking out her hand. "I live next door." She motioned with her head. "Well, my aunt and uncle live next door and I'm staying with them for a while."

"Hi." Tom took her hand. "I'm Tom Lovett. Nice to meet you." He noticed that her hand seemed kind of sweaty, and he was relieved to think she was probably as nervous as he was.

"Nice to meet you too." She gave his hand a slight squeeze before letting go.

An uncomfortable silence followed and Tom's mind raced, searching for something to say, but it was Madison who broke the silence.

"I saw you playing basketball yesterday," she confessed. "And I just thought it might be cool if I came over and introduced myself."

He was smiling again. *Say something, stupid,* he thought frantically.

"So you threw a Frisbee at me?"

Madison smiled slyly, shrugging. "Sorry. I kind of did it without thinking. I hope I didn't mess up your computer."

"It's okay," Tom said. "Sometimes I get the urge to throw things too."

They both laughed. "Do you want to sit down?" he asked her, gesturing toward the chairs set up around the patio table.

"Sure," she said, taking a chair close to his.

Tom sat back down. He glanced toward his laptop to see that the screen saver had activated: *Sports Illustrated* swimsuit models flashing by in a slide show. He quickly placed his finger on the mouse pad and the pictures were replaced by his essays.

"Nice screen saver," Madison said wryly.

"Yeah," Tom answered, feeling his cheeks flush. "I really need to get a new one." He realized that he was still holding on to the blue Frisbee and quickly handed it to her. "I think this belongs to you," he said, and she smiled as she took it from him.

"Thanks. I've been looking for this."

They laughed again, and she craned her neck to see what was displayed on the laptop screen.

"I'm nosy. Is this for school?"

Tom felt his heart beat faster. His mind raced, close to panic. Trying to explain the whole homeschooling thing and the reason why didn't seem to be an I-just-met-you conversation, especially with a hot girl.

"Yeah," Tom managed as he reached over and pulled down the screen. "Just wrapping up some stuff before the end of the year."

She nodded, and he breathed a sigh of relief.

"So, what year are you?"

"Um, junior."

"Me too," Madison said. "I finished up a little early so I could come out here."

"I thought I noticed an accent," Tom said. "Where are you from?"

"Chicago," Madison replied. "Born and raised. Ever been there?"

He shook his head. If it didn't involve his father's job, Tom's family didn't travel all that much; in fact, they didn't travel at all. "No, but I hear it's a lot like Boston."

"Way better than Boston," she said, with a wave of her hand that made him laugh.

"So how long are you here for?" Tom asked. "For the summer or . . . ?"

He stopped, noticing her face grow tense. Madison quickly looked away and began to fidget with a copper bracelet on her wrist. Great, he had somehow entered touchy territory. Now what?

Madison took a breath and looked back at him.

"That thing you're writing, it's something about John Steinbeck?" she asked, pointing to his laptop.

He lifted up the monitor screen again, grateful that the uncomfortable silence seemed to have passed. "Yeah," he said. "I was just finishing some essay questions on *The Grapes of Wrath*."

She looked thoughtful. "*Grapes of Wrath* was pretty good. Have you read any of his other stuff? *Cannery Row, Of Mice and Men, East of Eden*? I'd read *East of Eden* next if you haven't. My mom bought a copy because of that Oprah book club thing, and I needed something to read one day and thought it looked sort of interesting. It was really good. I wish I could write like that."

"So, you write? Like what, fiction?" he asked.

She shrugged. "Nothing major. I've done some short stories and some articles for my school paper."

"That's awesome," Tom said, truly impressed. At least her stuff had been read by somebody other than her parents.

"I was nominated for the Hemingway Awards for High School Journalists in the feature-writing category," Madison said. "But I didn't win," she added. "I lost to a story about this couple who raise monkeys to help disabled people."

Tom nodded. "At least you were nominated. That's pretty impressive."

She smiled and looked away. "Thanks. Do you write?"

"A little," he answered. "I couldn't win any awards or anything, but I occasionally like to write things down—y'know, get my thoughts on paper."

Tom was amazed. Just a few minutes ago he had been sitting alone, buried in schoolwork and thinking about an uncertain future, and now he was talking with a girl and feeling more normal than he had in a long, long time. It just went to show how quickly things could change.

Madison grinned. Tom seemed a little shy, maybe a little awkward, but there was something about him. She examined his face: his wide jawline, sandy blond hair, light blue eyes. She didn't want to stop looking at him. It was as though he gave off a kind of electricity that charged the air around him and yet was totally unaware of it.

A voice from the yard next door interrupted her thoughts.

"Madison?" she heard her aunt call. "Madison, are you out here?"

She glanced from Tom to the fence and back again.

"Somebody's looking for you," he said.

"It's my aunt—I've got to get going," Madison replied. "But it was great talking with you."

"Yeah," he agreed as she started to leave. "It was good to meet you too."

She waved and smiled, then turned and headed toward the fence she would have to climb to return to her own yard.

"Madison," she heard Tom call, and turned to see him snatch up the Frisbee from the patio table and jog across the yard to her. "You forgot this."

"Keep it," she said, hopping up onto the fence. "Gives me a reason to come back," she explained with a sly grin.

And she dropped down into her aunt and uncle's yard, already thinking about the next time she would see him again.

CHAPTER 5

Tom couldn't remember a time that his mother's meat loaf ever tasted so good, and he had to wonder if it had anything to do with the buzz he still felt after meeting Madison Fitzgerald.

He couldn't forget the image of her slowly walking away from him across the yard toward the back fence. *Wow.*

"You're quiet tonight." His mother intruded on his thoughts as she helped herself to another spoonful of mashed potatoes. "Is everything all right? Are you feeling okay?"

He chewed and swallowed before answering. "I'm fine. Just thinking about some stuff."

"Stuff?" his dad piped in. "And what kind of *stuff* are you thinking about? School *stuff*? Health *stuff*? What's on your mind? If there's a problem, maybe we can help you out."

His father often did this, barraging him with a hundred questions at once. Tom guessed that it was his way of keeping in touch with what was going on in his son's life, but it often felt more like an interrogation than a friendly father-and-son chat.

"No problems," Tom said, taking another bite of meat loaf. His father stared as he chewed.

"You know there's nothing you can't tell us, right?" he asked, pouring some more bottled water into his glass.

"Of course he does, Mason," his mom chimed in. She wiped her mouth with a paper napkin and dropped it onto her empty plate.

"Well, I know Tom's been having a hard time with things lately, and I just wanted to let him know that we're here if he needs us."

Tom smiled warmly at his father as he chewed the last of his green beans. "I know, Dad, and I appreciate it."

His father resumed eating as Tom scanned what remained of dinner. "Would anybody care if I had that last piece of meat?" he asked, already reaching for the plate.

"Help yourself," Victoria answered, helping him to move the plate closer.

"Knock yourself out," Mason added. "I've had plenty."

Everything was quiet then, his mom sipping her iced tea while his dad removed a small day planner from his back pocket and began making some notes on the calendar. Tom quietly continued to eat, his mind replaying his meeting with the girl next door.

"I met a girl today," he suddenly blurted. It just seemed to slip out.

"You did?" his mother asked, a smile slowly forming. "And where did you meet this girl?"

Dad closed the day planner, his attention piqued.

"In the yard," Tom told them as he picked up his napkin and swiped it over his mouth. "She threw a Frisbee and nearly scared the crap out of me."

"She threw a Frisbee at you?" his father asked. "What was she doing in the yard?"

"She came from next door," Tom explained. "Her name is Madison, and she's staying with her aunt and uncle."

"So she just showed up in our yard?" Victoria questioned. "When was this?"

"Today," he said. "This afternoon. I was doing some homework, and she hopped the fence to talk to me. She said she noticed me playing ball the other day and wanted to come over and introduce herself." He couldn't help but beam as he talked about her. "She's from Chicago. She's a writer."

"Sounds like she's something, don't you think?" his father asked his mother.

"She certainly does," Mom said cheerily. "I wasn't aware that there was somebody new living next door. Do you know how long she's staying?"

Tom shrugged. "I don't know."

Mason took the planner from the table and returned it to his back pocket. "So you think you'll be seeing her again?" he asked.

Tom played with his fork, crushing a sliver of green bean into paste. "Yeah, I hope so," he responded. "She left the Frisbee so she'd have to come back." He was smiling again. Maybe, just maybe he wasn't as big a freak as he thought he was.

"Well, I don't want this girl to become too much of a distraction for you," his father warned. "Remember, you have studies to maintain and there is your health to take into consideration."

Tom glared at his father, a flush of anger making his face feel hot. "I'm aware of my health."

"Now, Tom," his mother jumped in. "What your father is trying to say is—"

"I know what he's trying to say." Tom pushed back his chair. "He's saying, Don't forget, you're not normal."

Dad sighed, closing his eyes in exasperation. "That's

not what I said and you know it. I'm just cautioning you not to go overboard with this girl. You know nothing about her, and besides, she'll probably be gone by the end of summer anyway."

Tom stood up. "If you want me, I'll be upstairs."

"He didn't mean to upset you," his mother said, reaching out to take hold of his arm. "We just want you to be careful. We don't want to see you get hurt."

He was angry, and he knew he should escape before he said something that would get him into trouble. But he couldn't help himself.

"Y'know, you're always talking about how you don't want to see me sick or hurt and stuff, but you have no idea how it feels when you talk to me like this, like I'm some kind of special case that needs to be protected from the world."

Mason Lovett slowly crossed his arms over his chest, tilting his head slightly as he listened, waiting for Tom to cross the line.

"I was really excited today about meeting this girl, and do you know why? It wasn't just because she was really good looking and smart. What really excited me was the fact that she treated me like a normal guy. I wasn't "that kid with the narcolepsy": I was just Tom Lovett, a guy next door."

His mother had let go of his arm, and he turned to

walk from the kitchen. "That was really nice for the short time it lasted."

The workout helped him calm down some.

It was all part of his regular grind, a light workout three hours before bedtime. Sometimes he used the treadmill or the weight machine in the family room downstairs; other times he'd just shoot some baskets outside in the yard. Tonight he had used the weight machine until the muscles in his arms and legs burned from exertion.

A shower and then some downtime usually followed his exercise: maybe watching some television or a DVD or sometimes just surfing the Net. But tonight he couldn't concentrate on much. Tom's mind was filled with thoughts of Madison Fitzgerald.

He rubbed his wet hair roughly with a towel. Tom tossed the towel to the floor and stood in front of his dresser mirror, picking up a brush. He knew it was stupid to be obsessing about someone he hardly knew, but there was definitely something about Madison that he couldn't get off his mind.

Tom stared at his reflection in the mirror. The bruising on his forehead seemed as if it had already started to fade, and he wondered if it was even possible for somebody like Madison to be interested in him. He didn't think he was all that bad looking, but it wasn't his looks that were the problem. The fear of having an attack had kept him close to home, so his chances of meeting people his own age, especially girls, were pretty much zero.

He might really like this girl. Sure, she was attractive, and yes, she had talked to him—*the first girl his age he'd talked to in, like, three years*—but there was something more than that. He had felt a connection.

Tom went to the window, opening it a little wider. There was a breeze tonight, and the sound of the wind passing through the leaves was strangely soothing.

He stood at the window, hand ready to draw the shade, and looked across at the house next door. There were two lights on downstairs and one upstairs. He wondered if the upstairs light was in the room where Madison was staying.

"You're such a freak," he muttered, pulling the shade midway and returning to his bed.

He removed his watch and glasses and set them down on the bedside table as he did every night. He had always hated going to bed, even as a little boy— there was always a part of him that was afraid this would be the time he wouldn't wake up, that this night he would drift off and descend so far down into sleep that he couldn't find his way back to the waking world.

He pulled back the covers and crawled into bed, trying to push the unnerving thoughts from his mind. Reaching over to the nightstand, he switched off the lamp, plunging the room into semidarkness, illuminated only by the quarter moon in the night sky and the soft lights from the neighbors' house next door.

Madison's house.

Tom closed his eyes and braced himself for sleep, drifting off faster than he expected.

The hunter moved through the darkness as though he were a part of it.

Silently he cut through the nighttime woods, darting from tree to tree, steadily making his way toward the cabin sitting at the top of the rise.

The forest was quiet, unusually so, as if sensing his intent, as if knowing what he had come to do.

He made himself at home in any environment— crowded city streets, dense primordial jungle: it was all the same to him. He had a function to perform, a job to do, and he would finish it without hesitation.

From a place of concealment he studied the cabin— rustic in name only, he was certain. The structure was sure to be equipped with all the amenities of the modern home— the perfect place to escape the pressures of day-to-day life, to hide from the ills of the world.

With careful eyes he searched the darkness for any signs of security measures. Not finding any, he slowly moved toward the cabin, hugging the shadows, all of his senses completely focused on his surroundings.

The night remained silent, offering up no surprises as he climbed the three plank steps to the cabin's porch. He stood perfectly still, eyes closed, imagining the layout inside. He heard sounds from within and, using the blueprint drawn in his mind, figured they were coming from an area away from the door, allowing him to enter without being noticed. The hunter studied the door, then reached out and gripped the smooth metal of the doorknob. It turned easily and quietly.

It was nice on the inside, cozy. His eyes darted about the entryway, taking it all in. Its layout was almost exactly as he had imagined.

Slowly he followed the sound of activity, down the short corridor toward a room just beyond the cabin's entrance. The hunter carefully rounded the corner, peering into a room that could best be described as a den. His eyes immediately focused on a lone figure, kneeling on the wooden floor before a fireplace. He was an older man, with a head of thick white hair, wearing brown corduroys and a heavy cable-knit sweater; there were slippers on his feet. The fire burned low, and he was using a metal poker to move the logs around. A fresh pile of wood waited to his right.

The hunter said nothing and simply stood in the door-way, watching his prey work to rekindle the blaze. He had added the first of the new logs to the growing fire when his body suddenly froze. The hunter had seen this before in the hunted. It was as if a long-dormant sixth sense was suddenly activated, an animal instinct that warned of impending danger.

The old man slowly began to turn. "You have been expected," he said.

The hunter smiled.

A predator's smile.

Tom came awake fighting the urge to scream.

Something was wrong. Something was terribly, ter-ribly wrong.

He was soaking with sweat, his body trembling with the terror that now gripped him. His mind was racing, horrible staccato images flashing through his head as he attempted to calm himself down, to put his jumbled thoughts into some sort of order. *Was it just a really bad dream or one of my hallucinations?* he wondered.

Staring up at the familiar, flaking ceiling in the morning light, he tried to slow his racing heart, taking deep breaths—in through his nose and out through his mouth. He had a hard time remembering when he had ever felt so completely freaked.

This must be what it's like to have a heart attack, he thought, his heart hammering so hard that he thought it might just burst. He had been taught relaxation exercises by a number of his doctors over the years and struggled to remember some of their instructions. He was supposed to clear his mind, imagine his racing heart within his body, and then picture the frantically pulsing muscle gradually slowing as he breathed deeply and slowly. Tom inhaled, inflating his lungs to capacity, and then breathed out, the picture of the pumping heart in his mind beginning to match the sensations inside his chest. *That's it*, he reassured himself, finally beginning to feel some sort of control.

But that was short lived.

The vision of an old man suddenly exploded to life in his head. Tom gasped, his body suddenly rigid.

The old man, his face flushed and pink with exertion—or was it fear?—knelt before a roaring fireplace, the shock of snow white hair on his head waving in the air like some bizarre kind of underwater plant life.

"You have been expected," he said.

Tom screwed his eyes tightly shut, trying without success to force the bizarre imagery from his mind. Instead he watched as the man took hold of the arm of a chair nearby and forced himself to his feet. The old man's eyes were intense and filled with fear as he stared, it seemed, at Tom.

But how can that be?

Tom was certain he'd never seen the man before, but he felt a strange connection to him. Questions about the man's identity hung on Tom's lips as he lay in his bed, pummeled by the vision playing inside his head. He knew that it was best to simply allow the hallucination— or whatever it was—to run its course, so he surrendered to it, allowing it to play out to its conclusion.

The white-haired man looked like he was about to speak again when Tom heard a strange coughing sound and an explosion of red appeared on the front of the man's sweater. At first Tom wasn't sure exactly what he was seeing, but then he heard the odd sound for a second time and another eruption of red appeared on the old man, as though a flower, a crimson flower, had blossomed on his chest. But then the flowers began to drip, to ooze, leaving a trail on the man's front as he crumpled to his knees and fell to the floor before the fireplace.

Holy shit! Tom thought, realizing what was happening. The old man had been shot; before Tom's very eyes, he'd been shot.

Panicking, Tom tried to break the vision's hold on him, but the nightmare imagery held him tight.

He suddenly found himself within the hallucination, positioned over the injured old man, staring down into his paling face. Bubbles of blood accumulated at the corners of his wrinkled mouth, trailing down to stain his cheek. The old man's gaze was defiant and his lips trembled as he tried to speak.

Unable to control his actions, Tom moved closer, leaning his ear toward the dying man's mouth to hear what were certain to be his final words. The old man spoke, a single word that Tom could not comprehend.

Then a figure clad in black appeared, a gun in his hand, a silencer attached to its barrel. The murderer knelt carefully beside the old man's body, keeping his back to Tom as he pressed two fingers to the dead man's throat. Tom wanted to see the killer's face, wanted to see the kind of person who could so coldly murder a defenseless old man.

And as if reading his thoughts, the killer slowly stood and turned to face him. Tom gasped. He was painfully familiar with the shaggy blond hair, athletic build, high cheekbones, and pointy nose; after all, he'd seen them every day of his life.

The killer was himself.

The vision released its hold, and Tom was able to move again. He tossed back the covers and jumped from his bed, his body drenched in sweat, his brain on fire. Snatching up his glasses from the bedside table, he stumbled as he headed for the door to his room. The muscles and joints of his legs ached painfully. He must have worked out harder than he realized the night before.

Tom didn't want to be in his room any longer; he wanted to be away from this place where hallucinations of murder and murderers who wore his face threatened to make him insane. He threw open the door and lurched out into the hallway. Immediately he felt better, the air much fresher here than the staleness of his bedroom. Barefoot, he padded down the carpeted hall toward the stairs. The muscles in his legs were still sore, so he was careful to grab hold of the wooden banister as he descended to the ground floor.

He heard the sounds of morning television wafting through the house from the kitchen as he reached the foyer at the foot of the stairs. Besides the aching muscles of his legs, he noticed a painful emptiness in his stomach. Just the thought of eating was enough to get the juices inside his empty belly gurgling.

"What's for breakfast?" he called, trying to sound as normal as he could—trying his best to forget the disturbing imagery of the hallucinations he had just endured. He was hoping for bacon and eggs, maybe even some home fries, but would settle for a big bowl of oatmeal. The way his stomach was feeling, anything would taste perfectly fine.

"Tom?" his mother called out, getting up from the tiny kitchen table to meet him in the doorway. "How are you feeling?"

"I'm good," he told her. The violent images from his waking vision tried to force their way to the forefront, but he managed to hold them back. "I'm good. Just a little stiff."

Then he caught the look in his mother's eyes, a look of genuine concern, and a creeping realization gradually began to dawn. He looked to the watch that wasn't there.

"Oh no," he said, rubbing the skin on his wrist, feeling like he might be sick. He leaned against the doorway for support, his aching legs trembling.

"How long?" he asked, fearing the answer.

She placed a warm hand against his cheek. "You poor thing."

"How long, Mom?" he demanded, his voice cracking with emotion. He didn't want to hear it, but he had to.

"Five days," she whispered, looking away, not wanting to see the hurt in his eyes.

He felt the kitchen lurch around him as his legs gave way and he slid down the door frame to collapse on the cold kitchen floor.

"You've been asleep for five days."

CHAPTER 6

ALBANIA.
THE SOUTHERN PORT CITY OF VLORË.

The dilapidated warehouse stank of old fish and motor oil: odorous remnants of its past.

Brandon Kavanagh stepped up onto the makeshift stage and looked out over the vast space at those who were seated before it, waiting for what he had to show them.

Kavanagh smirked as he studied their faces: terrorists, weapons dealers, leaders of rogue nations. A veritable *Who's Who* of international criminals had answered his invitation. *What the CIA wouldn't give to be made privy to this little gathering,* Kavanagh mused as he eyed the crowd. One Patriot missile targeted on the warehouse and the war on terror would have been delivered a decisive blow—but that would have been bad for business.

"Good turnout," said a heavily accented voice from behind him, and Kavanagh turned to see a short, muscular man with dark hair and a bushy mustache entering the warehouse through a side door. The man smiled, removing a pack of cigarettes from his coat pocket.

"It appears that everyone who received an invitation has shown up," Kavanagh replied, leaving the makeshift stage. "Thank you again for the use of these lovely accommodations."

The man smiled again, offering a cigarette from his pack to Kavanagh, who politely refused. "More than happy to oblige a fellow businessman." He placed a cigarette in the corner of his mouth and set the tip ablaze with a gold lighter.

The swarthy man's name was Aleksander Berat, one of the most powerful figures in the Albanian underworld. At one time he had been chief of police in Vlorë, but then his brother had been killed in an ambush, and Berat had done what any enraged member of the Albanian justice system would have done. He'd resigned his post and gone on a murderous rampage, first killing a fellow policeman who was suspected of complicity in the murder and then eight others he believed to be responsible in some way. Nine deaths, one for every bullet hole in his brother's dead body.

"Then I take it you are satisfied with the fee?" Kavanagh asked.

Berat puffed twice on the cigarette, then removed it from his mouth so that he could speak. "Completely. But I must admit that I am curious as to why the payment was so much more than we originally agreed. Perhaps you are simply a generous man, Mr. Kavanagh?" He returned the cigarette to his lips and waited for an answer.

Kavanagh smiled. "Generous? Not overly, but definitely cautious. The extra amount is to guarantee your silence and that of your employees." He again looked out over the crowded room, feeling the crackle of anticipation hanging heavy in the fetid air. "No one must know of this demonstration." He turned back to the former police chief. "What you see here tonight stays in this room; do I make myself clear, Mr. Berat?"

Berat finished his cigarette and dropped its smoldering remains to the warehouse floor. "Crystal," he replied, snuffing out the embers with the toe of his Italian loafer. "Albania is a place of many secrets," he said with a snarl of a smile. "But of course you already know that, for why else would you have chosen it for your exhibition?"

"Just so we understand each other, Mr. Berat," Kavanagh said, an air of threat hidden beneath the cover of civil conversation.

Aleksander Berat was not a man to be trifled with. It was said that when his brother was murdered, Aleksander died as well, and something inhuman now lived inside the shell of the former police officer. But Brandon Kavanagh was far from average himself and had spent a great deal of his professional life dealing with people like Berat. Kavanagh wouldn't think twice about eliminating this man, his family, and his business associates if ever they threatened his own interests.

The two men momentarily locked eyes and an understanding passed quietly between them.

"It must be quite an item you are selling," Berat said, breaking the silence. "Something very dangerous if it has attracted the likes of them." He gestured with his head toward the gathering. "Something expensive."

Kavanagh glanced quickly at his watch. "Let us hope," he said, reaching inside his coat pocket for a cell phone. He punched a preprogrammed number into the phone and waited momentarily. "It's time," he spoke into it, then broke the connection and returned it to his pocket.

The side door opened again and a man came in, escorting a pretty, dark-haired girl, no older than thirteen. She was wide-eyed with fear as the man took her arm and pulled her toward the stage.

"Is that what you are selling, my friend?" Berat asked, a chuckle rumbling deep within his throat. "I could sell you four just like her with one phone call."

Kavanagh smiled. "I seriously doubt that," he replied. "Have your men secure the building."

Berat sighed, shaking his head as he signaled to his men stationed around the warehouse. They immediately began to padlock the entrances.

Kavanagh could see apprehension beginning to appear on the faces of his clientele and he stepped back onto the stage to reassure them. "Please." He raised his voice to be heard from the wooden platform. "There's no need for concern. This is simply a precautionary measure."

A buzz went up from the crowd and Kavanagh reveled in its intensity. He had been waiting a long time for this moment.

Someone handed him a cordless microphone. "Can you all hear me?" he asked, his voice amplified by twin speakers placed on either side of the stage. "Excellent. First, I would like to thank you all for coming. I hope that you will find what I have to offer as valuable as I believe it to be."

He studied the faces of those in the crowd, many reflecting skepticism, but he knew that would not be the case for long. "But I'll let you decide," he continued. "Shall we begin?"

He turned to the man standing beside the teenage

girl and nodded. The man gripped the girl's arm and pulled her to center stage, where he positioned her beneath spotlights that had been rigged from the ceiling. Despite the damp conditions, the girl was dressed in a short denim skirt and a sleeveless T-shirt, and her teeth chattered as she looked about the cavernous room. Not entirely from the cold, Kavanagh imagined.

"This is Amy," he said into the microphone. "She is thirteen years old, five-foot five, one hundred and four pounds soaking wet." He smiled at his irreverence, certain that his audience was on the verge of losing their patience with him. "Say hello to the nice people who have come to meet you, Amy," he said to the frightened girl, and held out his microphone so that she could be heard.

"Hello," she squeaked, her voice trembling with fear.

A man in the crowd, who Kavanagh recognized as Salim Yasir, a weapons dealer, suddenly stood. "What is the meaning of this?" he raged. "You promised a weapon and you present to us a frightened child? I will be a part of this foolishness no longer." He started to leave, two bodyguards in tow.

"Wait," Kavanagh commanded. "Just another moment of your time. I'm sure you will not be disappointed."

Yasir turned and glared at him, then at the others in

attendance, and realized that he was the only one prepared to depart.

"I will give you fifteen minutes," he said haughtily,
throwing himself into his seat, arms folded across his
chest, daring Kavanagh to impress him.

"Now, where were we?" Kavanagh returned his
attention to the teenage girl. "Ah, yes, Amy."

She flinched as if struck.

"Are you afraid, Amy?" he asked.

The girl nodded, looking like she was on the brink
of tears.

"I'm sorry for that," he told her, sounding most
sincere. "And I'm sorry for what I'm about to do now."

Kavanagh raised a hand and six men moved forward
from where they had stood within the shadows at the
edge of the platform. They had been another service
bought from Aleksander Berat—six of the most vile,
twisted men in Albania. Berat had used his connections
in the police force to choose from a variety of monsters
serving time in Albania's archaic correctional system.

The six joined Kavanagh on the stage, and he knew
that Berat had done his job well as they stared at him
with dark, dead eyes devoid of any human emotion.
They were animals. All they knew was that they were to
be paid this evening for a reprehensible act, and they
were more than happy to oblige.

"Do you see that girl?" Kavanagh asked them. He pointed to her with his microphone. "I want you to hurt her. I want you to make her wish that she had never been born."

They grinned like sharks and slowly made their way toward her.

Amy turned to run, but Kavanagh stopped her with a single command. "Stay where you are."

She trembled uncontrollably, her cheeks stained with tears as the six monsters circled her like hungry hyenas closing in on defenseless prey.

"Are you frightened, Amy?" Kavanagh asked into the microphone.

"Yes!" she shrieked, frantically swatting at the men's groping hands. The criminals were laughing now, amused by her terror.

Kavanagh turned his attention to his audience. "Watch," he commanded.

Amy had fallen to her knees, burying her face in her hands as the six men closed in around her. Casually glancing over to the side of the stage, Kavanagh saw that Berat looked like he was going to jump from his skin. The Albanian was sweating profusely, eyes wide in shock. *Not such a monster after all, eh, Aleksander?* Kavanagh observed, now ready to begin the true demonstration.

He removed the phone from his pocket once again, punched in some numbers, waited a heartbeat, and then spoke. "Activate," he said, a smile of excitement threatening to dispel his serious expression.

He carefully watched his audience, wanting to see their reaction, to feel the vast room thrum with excitement as they saw what he was offering them.

"Are you still afraid, Amy?" he asked, without turning toward her.

"No," replied a voice no longer trembling with fear.

"Then show me."

And he listened to the sounds of violence that suddenly erupted from behind him: sounds of skulls being fractured, of limbs yanked from their sockets, of bones snapping like pieces of dry wood. Of grown men begging not to be hurt.

Brandon Kavanagh did not have to turn around to know what was happening on the stage behind him, nor did he have to hear the screams of six dying men. All that he needed he saw in the eyes of his audience and in the stupefied expressions on their faces.

And he basked in the recognition of his genius.

CHAPTER 7

The June sun felt awesome on Madison's bare skin.

It was the first day that made her honestly believe summer really was just around the corner, and she wanted to take full advantage of the beautiful day.

Madison reclined on a lounge chair in her aunt and uncle's backyard, wearing her favorite bikini top, a pair of gray shorts, and sunscreen, basking in the rays of the afternoon sun. She was in that bizarre place, not asleep, but not fully awake either. Some of her best thinking had been done in this weird in-between state, and at the moment her mind was preoccupied with thoughts of the last week.

A shadow moved across her eyelids, and her skin felt suddenly cooler. She was waiting for the cloud to pass when somebody cleared his throat.

"What!" she said with a start, shocked to open her eyes to find a figure standing over her.

"Sorry," Tom Lovett said, shrugging and stepping back.

Madison grabbed a button-down dress shirt from the ground beside her chair and slipped it on over her bare shoulders, suddenly shy. "How long have you been standing there?" she asked.

"Not long," he answered. "I wasn't sure if you were asleep. I didn't want to scare you."

"Yeah, right," she joked. "You just wanted to get me back for the Frisbee incident last week."

He laughed, and she noticed that he had a really nice smile.

"Hey, are you sure you should be over here?" She looked past him to the fence.

"Why?" He looked confused. "Do your aunt and uncle have rules about you being alone with guys?"

"No," she said, waving his suggestion away. "It's just that I went by your house the day after we talked and your mother said you weren't up for visitors and I haven't seen you since."

Tom moaned aloud and ran his fingers through his hair, dropping down to sit in the grass in front of her chair.

"I thought it was an interesting way of blowing me off." She shrugged. "Having your mom do it for you and all."

"Oh God, it's not that," he said. He buried his face in his hands. "It's not that at all."

"Hey, I was only joking," Madison said quickly. She extended her leg and playfully tapped his shoulder with her bare foot. "What's wrong?"

Tom looked up at her, and the expression on his face was very serious. Behind his glasses his blue eyes had become intense. "See, I have this condition," he started to explain. "And it makes my mother a little overprotective sometimes."

"Condition?" Madison leaned forward in the lounge chair. "What, like you're sick or something?"

Tom shrugged, looking at the ground and picking at a blade of grass. "Yeah, sort of. I have narcolepsy," he said. "I've had it since I was a kid."

"Isn't that like the disease where you fall asleep for no reason?" she asked.

He nodded, looking very uncomfortable.

"Oh, crap," Madison blurted, surprised at how relieved she suddenly felt. "Is that all? I can fall asleep just about anywhere; maybe I've got it too." She made a goofy face and pretended to be dozing off.

But Tom wasn't laughing.

"I'm sorry," Madison apologized. "Sometimes I speak before I think. I didn't mean to hurt your feelings."

He shook his head, still not looking at her. "No, that's all right. I'm just a little sensitive about it is all. I probably shouldn't have said anything."

He fell silent then, playing with the grass on the ground in front of him, and Madison realized what a big deal it must have been for him to tell her this.

"So, you've had this . . . condition since you were little?" she asked hesitantly.

Tom had pulled up a long blade of grass and was carefully tying it into knots. "Yeah, I had my first attack when I was eight."

"That must have been tough." She wasn't sure what to say but wanted him to know that she was trying to be understanding.

He nodded. "Oh yeah, all the tests and stuff. It was pretty scary for a little kid." He quickly glanced up from his knotted piece of grass. "You can see where Mom and Dad would be kinda smothering. I've put them through quite a bit."

She moved to the end of the lounge chair, closer to him, fascinated with the idea that this healthy-looking teenage boy could have something dramatically wrong with him. "I don't want to be rude," she said carefully. "But what's it like?"

He looked hard at the ground, thinking about the best way to answer. "It's not fun, that's for sure," he finally said. "I wish I could say you get used to it over time, but you don't. It's like somebody has a switch for your life and is turning it on and off whenever they feel like it. It makes you angry that you're so goddamned helpless."

Madison resisted the urge to put her arm around his shoulders to comfort him. She could sense his frustration and found herself empathizing with him. Life itself wasn't so bad; it was the curveballs it threw every once in a while that caused all the problems.

"Is there any medicine you can take?"

"Yeah, lots of medication," he said, "but no cure. The medicine just helps keep the attacks to a minimum—that and a regular routine of exercise and naps." He chuckled sadly. "Pretty pathetic, huh?"

Madison shook her head and reached out to take the knotted piece of grass from his hands. "Not pathetic at all," she tried to reassure him. "You do what you do to stay well. If you had allergies, you'd take medicine for that, right?"

Tom laughed. "I never thought of narcolepsy as an allergy, but when you put it that way, I guess you're right." He looked at her and smiled. "Thanks."

"Don't mention it." She playfully threw the knotted blade of grass at him, attempting to lighten the conversation. And then it dawned on her. As she stared at his handsome, smiling face, she realized why she hadn't seen him for a while. "Oh my God," she said. "Your mom said you weren't around, but you were—"

"Asleep," Tom interrupted, finishing her sentence. "I had an attack that night after we met. It was a bad one, the worst since I was diagnosed with Quentin's. I lost five days."

"Quentin's?" she questioned. "Is that a *kind* of narcolepsy?"

"Named after the guy who discovered it, I guess," Tom explained. "Lucky me, it's a more-rare form. Most narcoleptic seizures take you out of the picture for ten, twenty minutes—an hour max. But Quentin's is a whole other story." Tom rose to his feet, brushing off the seat of his sweatpants. "I just broke my last record. Who knows, maybe I can get it recognized by the Olympic committee and get a gold medal."

"It scares you, doesn't it?" she said suddenly.

Tom chuckled, and for a moment Madison thought he might joke about it. But then he hung his head and turned away, and she knew he was speaking from his heart.

"Yeah, it does. Sometimes I'm afraid to go to sleep at night because I think I might not wake up."

He gazed down at her, and they were quiet for a moment.

"I was thinking," he started, quickly changing the subject, glancing over at the fence and his yard beyond it. "How about coming over for dinner tomorrow night?"

She didn't have to think about the answer. "Sure, that'd be great. Your mother's going to let me in the house this time?" she asked sarcastically.

"Don't worry about her." Tom laughed reassuringly. "I'll make sure she's on her best behavior."

It was well past midnight, but Tom didn't want to go to sleep. He had lost five days to unconsciousness, and he didn't feel that it deserved any more of his life right now.

He was sitting on his bed, computer in his lap, searching the Internet. *What was the name of that award she was nominated for?* he asked himself, fingers paused over the plastic keys. *Ernest Hemingway*, he remembered, typing the author's name into the search engine.

Tom knew he was pushing his luck. He hadn't bothered to work out or nap during the day. His parents would probably say he was rebelling against his illness again, but the explanation was much simpler. He really was afraid—afraid of his dreams. Bizarre images from the hypnagogic hallucination he'd had the other night flashed through his mind, and he felt that disconcerting tingle at the back of his neck as the hair there stood on end. He'd had many hallucinations, but none had ever stayed with him like this one.

He saw the old man again, the flowers of blood blossoming on his chest as he fell backward to the fireplace hearth. Tom rubbed vigorously at his eyes, trying to make the images of the dying man disappear—the man that he had killed.

No. He hadn't killed anyone; it was only a dream. A screwed-up dream.

He reached over to his nightstand for the open can of Coke. Another big-time no-no, caffeine before bed, but he didn't care—it helped to keep him awake.

"Okay, where was I?" He took a deep breath and focused his attention back on the laptop. *This must be it,* he thought, clicking on the site for the Ernest Hemingway Writing Awards for High School Journalists."

He was curious if the site had any work posted from the people who had been nominated. Luckily it did, including the year Madison was nominated. He found her name with three others under the heading Runners-up and called up her entry. He was thinking he might be able to impress her by talking about the article at dinner tomorrow night.

Dinner. Crap. He'd forgotten to tell his mother about their guest, and he briefly toyed with the idea of going to tell her now. *Nah,* he decided. She'd probably already be asleep and then mad that he was still awake. *I'll tell her in the morning,* he decided, and went back to Madison's article.

It was a piece on a small nursing home in Chicago and how its residents had become their own extended family, doing their best to care for each other, offering support and sharing families with those residents who didn't have any. The story was really well written, and he wondered how it could possibly have been beaten out by an article on monkeys, but then again, he *was* slightly biased.

Tom's mind started to wander as the image of Madison lying out in her bikini top took over front and center. Pretty much where it had been since he'd seen her earlier.

He was smiling when explosions of crimson suddenly blasted through the image. An old man's withered mouth rose up from the sea of thick red, struggling to speak. To say the word that Tom had not been able to hear during last night's hallucination.

"Janus," said the mouth as it filled with blood, and the crimson liquid became like an ocean swallowing up the trembling maw before it could speak again, and everything turned to red.

The sensation of the computer sliding from his lap was enough to pull Tom from the grip of the bloody vision, and he caught it just as it was about to fall over the edge of his bed. His breath was coming in quick, labored gasps and his heart beat incredibly fast as he carefully placed the laptop safely down on the bed beside him. Hallucinations had been a part of his life for nearly as long as he could remember, generally bizarre, sometimes disturbing. And he had learned to live with them, riding them out until they were finished or until he could manage to break their hold on him. But there was something about these latest visions that he found absolutely terrifying. These were different, almost real.

"Janus," he said aloud, trying out the word. The smell of blood was suddenly in his nostrils, and Tom wanted to gag. He had read once that intense hallucinations and unexplained smells were the first signs of a brain tumor and wondered if that was the answer to recent events.

Janus. He couldn't get the word out of his mind. It echoed inside his head, the old man's voice wet with blood.

Tom glanced at the laptop beside him and quickly picked it up, typing the mysterious name into the same search engine he'd used to locate Madison's article. The results were typical, ranging from computer software companies to porn sites. He scanned the length of the page until his eyes landed on something different. It was a description from a site dedicated to world myths and legends, where he learned that Janus was a lesser god of Roman mythology. He clicked on the site to learn more.

Janus was the Roman god of gates and doors, he read, beginnings and endings, represented by a double-faced head, each looking in opposite directions. Tom scrolled down the page until he came to a photograph of a statue of the god. He focused on the two faces. Both were the same, but one wore a look of calm, the other an expression of ferocity.

For a moment Tom felt himself begin to slip away, like he was about to be sucked into another of his bizarre visions. Instead his fingers began typing, seemingly on their own, and he was calling up a site that he'd had no previous knowledge of.

The site downloaded and a picture of a heavy wooden door appeared on his screen, the kind of door that might be found on a log cabin. A haunting piece of classical music began to play, startling him.

A blank window appeared beneath the picture of the door, where a password was supposed to be entered. Tom stared at the space, and suddenly the Latin word for *truth* inexplicably popped into his head. Feeling the slightest twinge of fear, he typed *veritas* into the space and then hit enter.

The screen went blank, and his modem began to make bizarre noises. *Shit,* he thought, hitting the escape key, hoping he hadn't just opened the door to some nasty virus that would destroy his hard drive. He hit escape again just for good measure. What was he thinking? How could he have done something so . . .

The screen blinked out momentarily, and then a video began to play. Tom gasped, hypnotized by the image of the old man from his dream, sitting in a high-backed leather chair before a roaring fireplace, a red blanket draped over his legs. The old man was looking at him, a warm smile on his grandfatherly features.

"Hello, Tom," the man said. "If you've found this, then it means that I am dead, and things have been set in motion that cannot be permitted to continue."

Tom felt like he was being electrocuted, raw voltage coursing through his body, holding him in place. He couldn't take his eyes off the computer screen—off the old man.

"First, let me assure you, this is not a product of your illness but the beginning of a process that will reveal to you the truth and set you free. There are things you must know about yourself, Tom, things that have been hidden from you."

Tom began to panic, terrified that he was losing his mind. His finger moved toward the power button.

"You must listen carefully to me, Tom," the mysterious old man cautioned. "I need you to sleep."

Tom tried to hit the power button, but his limbs suddenly weighed hundreds of pounds, and he found that he could no longer keep his eyes open. "No," he gasped, his chin lolling down to touch his chest.

"That's it, Tom," the old man was saying. "Nice and easy."

Tom fought hard but was pulled deeper and deeper.

"There is so much to tell you." The old man's voice followed him into the realm of dreams. "Soon it will all be revealed. But first, sleep. Go ahead, Tom, just let yourself sleep."

CHAPTER 8

Christian Tremain's hand shook uncontrollably as he brought the coffee cup to his lips, its contents spilling over the rim and down his chin, staining his tie.

"It's going to be one of those days," he grumbled, cursing under his breath as he placed the cup into the holder and searched the glove compartment for napkins. He found three and dabbed at the wet spots dappling the surface of his navy blue silk tie, hoping the subdued yellow checks would hide the stains.

Tremain tossed two of the crumpled napkins into the paper bag that had once contained his coffee and again reached for the cup. His hand still shook.

Carefully he lifted the coffee to his mouth again, clutching the third napkin in his other hand just in case. Tremain watched the rain fall outside his car—the precipitation so heavy that the drains in the parking lot of the Lancelot Psychiatric Facility were having difficulty keeping up.

He didn't want to get out of the car—not because of the rain; the sun could be shining for all he cared. He just didn't think he had the strength for another day.

What choice do you have? a voice somewhere in the back of his thoughts asked. *This is your job—your responsibility. Think of the lives that could be lost if you were to fall down on the job.*

Christian Tremain sipped his hot drink, watching the rain and remembering how he had come to be here.

They had recruited him from the CIA's clandestine operations department, where he'd always imagined he would grow old and eventually retire. They called themselves the Pandora Group, and they'd piqued his curiosity the moment they made contact. They were a covert government agency working outside the constraints of the political machine: an agency in charge of the research and development of new technologies used to keep this great country safe.

The rain continued to pound the roof of his car in a frantic, staccato beat. His coffee was nearly cold, but still he drank, the final sips of the beverage bitter on his tongue.

Pandora was what intelligence agencies referred to

as a black box operation, with monies filtered in from any number of legitimate federally funded programs. Tremain had always wondered about the Pentagon's two-thousand-dollar toilet seats and the hundred thousand dollars spent by the air force to study the effect of the noise of jet engines on horses. Now he knew that this money was actually going to Pandora.

Why the secrecy? he was sure the average citizen would ask, and he would have to answer that occasionally things operatives within the group had to do were, well, viewed as amoral. So Pandora worked in secret, keeping the world safe from bad guys—at least that was what he'd told himself during his first years with the organization.

Tremain realized that his cup was empty and dropped it inside the bag on the passenger seat. The rain had diminished to a heavy mist, and he knew he could no longer put off his latest assignment.

Five years ago they had promoted him to the position of director of operations. It was supposed to be a cushy job, sitting in a big office in Washington behind an equally impressive desk, signing his name to documents authorizing programs that would keep this country safe. But he didn't see it that way. He wanted to know what was being done in the name of science—in the name of protecting the citizens of the United

States. And what he had seen in his five years as director had changed him dramatically.

Biological warfare, nanotechnology, genetic engineering, advanced robotics, weather manipulation: these were but a smattering of the fields being mined by groups working under the umbrella of the Pandora Group. What he had seen at some of these facilities had chilled him to the soul; the destructive potential of these sciences, should they be released upon the world, was mind-numbingly horrific.

And Tremain had made it his personal mission to see that that never happened.

He opened the car door and got out into the heavy mist. It was incredibly humid in West Virginia this time of year, and he debated whether to leave his raincoat behind but decided against it, slamming his car door closed and making his away across the parking lot to the building's front entrance.

The Lancelot Psychiatric Facility had been closed for over twenty years, and the public believed the building now housed a research group searching for a cure for autism. *If only that were the case,* Tremain thought as he slowly climbed the concrete steps to the front doors. Actually it was home to one of Pandora's most intriguing endeavors, the Janus Project.

At the top of the stairs he pushed an intercom button.

"Yes?" came a cheerful-sounding voice from the mounted speaker.

"Christian Tremain to see Brandon Kavanagh," he said. A gust of moist wind made him pull up the collar of his raincoat. He was glad he had decided to wear it.

"Very good, sir," the pleasant voice responded, and a buzz sounded as the electronic lock disengaged.

The waiting area was painted a soft shade of green, and its calming atmosphere reminded him of a doctor's office. A door opened to the right of an empty reception desk, and an attractive older woman entered the room, accompanied by two large men. She smiled as she walked toward him. "If we could see some identification, please," she said pleasantly.

"Of course," Tremain responded. He pulled his wallet out of his suit coat, flipped it open, and handed it to her.

"Thank you, Mr. Tremain," she said with a gracious smile, folding up the wallet and handing it back to him. "Follow me, please." She gestured back toward the door behind her.

She punched in a code on a keypad beside the door. The two silent men walked at a polite distance behind them as they proceeded down a brightly lit corridor into the body of the facility. They took a right and came to another locked door with a small security camera mounted above it. Tremain listened to the faint hum of its pivoting mechanism as it trained its focus on them.

"Mr. Tremain, sir," the woman said, gazing up into the small electronic eye.

Tremain looked up as well, imagining Kavanagh on the other side, scrutinizing his appearance, attempting to read his body language, eager for some inkling as to why he had requested this meeting.

Brandon Kavanagh had been with Pandora for about as long as Tremain had. In fact, the two men had served together on an acquisitions committee, before his own appointment as director and Kavanagh's to the Janus Project. It had been several years since they had seen each other. Tremain remembered his old acquaintance as arrogant and frighteningly brilliant but was having a great deal of difficulty recalling any of the man's likable qualities.

The door unlocked with another electronic buzz and the woman pulled it open so that he could enter. "Down the hall and to your left," she directed.

He thanked her and walked down the short hallway until he came to a door on the left, slightly ajar. He rapped on the door frame with his knuckle before entering.

"Come in," called a voice from inside, and Tremain did.

He stepped into the spacious office and observed Kavanagh on the phone behind his desk. The man looked pretty much as he remembered, except for the nearly white hair, now worn extremely short.

Tremain looked around the office. It was nice, much nicer than his own back at operations. The dark wood paneling, track lighting, and framed artwork on the walls created a soothing environment. He noticed a coatrack in the corner and hung his rain-soaked coat on one of its hooks just as Kavanagh finished up his conversation.

"Sorry about that, Chris," Kavanagh said, leaning down to jot something on a notepad on the desk. "I'm surprised they can go to the bathroom without me to show them how it's done." He tossed down the pen and came around the desk, hand extended. "It's great to see you." A smile lit his handsome features. "It's been a long time."

Tremain took Kavanagh's hand and they shook. "It has, hasn't it," he answered politely. If he had managed never to see the man again in his lifetime, it wouldn't have fazed him in the least.

"Please, have a seat," Kavanagh said gesturing toward a leather chair in front of his desk as he went around to the other side. "I was a bit surprised to hear that you were coming down," he said, settling into his chair. "But at the same time a little excited. I think Pandora is going to be quite pleased with the advances we've made over the last six months."

A knock sounded at the door, and the assistant entered carrying a tray with coffee. The men thanked her, and she left with a radiant smile. "If you gentlemen need anything else, just call."

"I don't know what I'd do without Karen," Kavanagh said as he reached down and pulled a bottle of whisky from his bottom desk drawer. "Can I spice up your coffee a bit?" he asked with a wry smile.

There was nothing Tremain wanted more. Hell, he would have preferred to dump the coffee and just have the whisky, but that wasn't how it was now. As much as he craved it, he didn't drink anymore.

"No thank you," he replied, bringing his cup to his mouth, struggling to suppress the tremble.

"Are you sure?" Kavanagh enticed him. "It's Glenfiddich."

Tremain had been sober for six months and for six months able to think clearly. He didn't want to go back to the way things had been: looking at his life—his job—as if from a distance.

He shook his head as he placed his cup down on the saucer. "This is perfectly fine, thanks."

"Suit yourself." Kavanagh returned the whisky to

the drawer. "As I was saying, you won't be leaving here disappointed." He reached out and picked up a small remote control from the desktop, pointing to the wall behind him.

There was a faint hum and the wall slowly began to split open, revealing rows of television monitors. Multiple images appeared on the various screens. "As you can see, we're quite busy here," Kavanagh said proudly.

Tremain sipped his coffee as he studied each monitor. Scenes of incredible violence suddenly erupted on each of screens, startling him, hitting him like a slap across the face. He had already reviewed the files on Janus and knew that the project *had* made substantial advances. But this, it only made what he had come to do all the more pressing.

"You *have* been busy," he said, leaning forward to place his cup and saucer on the corner of Kavanagh's desk. "Which makes what I'm about to tell you so troubling."

Kavanagh quickly looked away from the screens. "I don't like the sound of that," he said, picking up the remote again and turning off the monitors.

"Reports have surfaced that allege that certain technologies developed here at Janus have found their way onto the black market," Tremain said, watching his former associate's face very closely.

"Impossible," Kavanagh scoffed. "Our security here is state of the art."

Tremain folded his hands in his lap, afraid that they might start to tremble again. "In Albania a teenage girl was put up for sale," he stated. "A teenage girl with the ability to take down six grown men with her bare hands." He paused for effect. "Do you believe this is a freak coincidence, Brandon?"

Kavanagh moved his coffee cup around on its saucer but had yet to drink. "Can you guarantee the validity of the report?" he asked, without looking up.

"Aleksander Berat has been a credible source of intelligence to the group for years. There's no reason to doubt him."

Kavanagh slowly raised his eyes and fixed Tremain with an intense stare. Tremain remembered those eyes well and the murderous efficiency that was often behind their ferocity.

"Did he provide us with the identity of whoever was behind the sale?"

Tremain slowly shook his head. "No. He did give us a vague description, but we believe the person who ran the show might have just been a middleman hired to negotiate the sale."

Kavanagh leaned back in his seat, rubbing one of his hands across his closely cropped white hair. "This is horrible," he said, staring up at the ceiling as if searching for answers from some divine source. "I can't believe this has happened." He was silent for a moment, then asked, "How should we proceed?" Tremain knew he had been in the business far too long not to know.

"I'm recommending that the Janus Project be terminated," Tremain said. "I'm sorry, Brandon, but protocol dictates that any breach of security must be—"

Kavanagh raised a hand to silence him. "I know what protocol dictates, Chris," he said coldly. "But what about the work? The years I've put into the project; what about that?"

Tremain sighed as he stood up from his chair. "You know Pandora," he said. "The work won't go to waste—it'll be absorbed into another project."

He turned to retrieve his coat as Brandon Kavanagh silently brooded about the fate of his work. "You know if there was any other way," Tremain began, slipping into his raincoat. It was still damp and the clammy feeling of the material sent a discomforting chill down his spine—at least, he *thought* it was the feeling of dampness.

"How long do I have?" Kavanagh asked flatly.

"I'll begin the paperwork as soon as I get back to operations, sometime tomorrow," he answered. "A data retrieval team will collect all pertinent information shortly thereafter. I'd recommend any evidence of your work here be erased by the end of the week. I'm really sorry about this, Brandon," Tremain added, stepping to the edge of the desk and extending his hand. "But there's too much of a risk, and I shudder to think of the ramifications."

Kavanagh stood slowly, accepting Tremain's hand. "Let's hope that we can find whoever was responsible for the Albanian display and nip it in the bud."

"That's our intention. We already have a team of our best people working on it."

"Excellent." Kavanagh released Tremain's hand. "Until we meet again."

"Good to see you, Brandon," Tremain said politely as he headed for the door.

Brandon Kavanagh sat behind his desk, about to set the plans for his future in motion.

The meeting with Tremain had not come as a complete surprise. The potential of his employer discovering the Albanian presentation had always been a possibility. And it was only a matter of time before they learned that he was responsible.

He leaned back in his chair and sighed. He would hate to leave this office, this facility, but he had no choice now. His role in life was about to change, and he felt a sensation of electric excitement raise the hair on the back of his neck and arms.

Noticing the untouched coffee on his desktop, he sat forward in his seat and carefully picked up the cup. The coffee was cold, but he still drank it.

Kavanagh had always seen himself as one of the good guys but knew that it wasn't a long journey to the other side. He had seen many things in his years trying to keep the world safe, things that often made him question whether or not it was even worth the struggle.

As much as he hated to admit it, he knew they were losing the battle, the world sliding deeper and deeper into chaos with every passing day. Really, what difference did it make which side he was on? Wasn't evil all a matter of perception anyway?

Evil. He smiled at his use of the word. It always sounded so dramatic, corny even.

Tremain's coming here was actually a blessing of sorts, a merciful end to a life hurtling toward the inevitable. Brandon Kavanagh had been straddling the line between good and evil for more years than he cared to think about, finding it more and more difficult with every passing year to tell one from the other. Today he had made the decision to cross over for good, and it wasn't as traumatic as he had imagined it would be.

He chuckled out loud. He shouldn't have been

surprised, really. Even when he was just a child, the villains in movies and on television interested him more than the heroes. His desire to see the bad guys win had always been his own little secret.

Brandon Kavanagh's life was full of secrets.

He stood and stretched, then removed his cell phone from his belt and flipped open the lid. Humming an odd tune, he punched a number into the keypad and placed the phone to his ear.

"It's me," he said. "I'm going to need you to wake up our friend." He moved out from behind his desk. "Yes, I'm aware that we've used him recently, but I need him again."

Kavanagh paused mid-office. "That's right. A wakeup call for Sleeper One. I'd like him to meet an old friend of mine."

He was about to hang up when he remembered something else, a matter of betrayal. "Oh yes, another thing. Kindly see to it that our Albanian friend and his associates meet with an unpleasant fate."

Kavanagh smiled. He really got a kick out of being a bad guy.

Tom glanced up at the kitchen clock and saw that it was nearly time for his guest to arrive.

"I'm setting another place," he warned his mother, who was busy at the stove.

"What do you mean?" she asked, turning from the sink with a steaming pan of broccoli in hand.

She had prepared a roast chicken for tonight's dinner. That, plus broccoli, salad, and fresh bread from Giordano's Bakery, made for what he thought was a perfectly acceptable meal—nothing embarrassing, like that tuna surprise with the egg cooked in the middle. Disgusting.

As if on cue there was a knock at the front door, and Tom watched as the look of confusion on his mother's features grew more pronounced.

"I invited a friend over for supper," he explained as he headed for the door.

"You did what?" she asked, voice slightly raised in agitation.

"I meant to mention it earlier, but I forgot. I didn't think you'd mind."

Tom hadn't really forgotten; it had been practically all he could think about the entire day. He hadn't mentioned it because he'd been afraid she'd say no, especially the way she'd been acting lately.

His mother was sputtering something from the kitchen behind him as he opened the front door and stopped cold. Madison stood on the porch, dressed in a short denim skirt and a fitted white button-down shirt. Her red hair fell in sexy waves past her shoulders. Tom was struck speechless.

"Hey," he finally managed, opening the door wider to let her in. "Thought you might've come over the fence and in the back way."

She laughed. "I could if you want," she suggested, pretending to leave.

"That's all right," he said, closing the door behind her.

"Well, there's always next time," she said, the slightest hint of a smile playing on her lips as their eyes momentarily locked.

Tom pulled his eyes from hers and escorted her toward the kitchen, keeping his fingers crossed that his parents would be on their best behavior.

"Mom, Dad, this is Madison Fitzgerald," he said. "She's the girl I told you about who's staying next door with her aunt and uncle."

Tom watched as his father quickly glanced at his mother, a comical look of bewilderment on his face.

"Hello," his mother responded with a nervous wave. "I'm Victoria and this is Mason."

It was his dad's turn to smile and wave. "Hi," he said, casually leaning on the countertop, trying not to look flustered. "Nice to meet you."

"Thanks so much for having me over," Madison said.

"You're welcome," Victoria replied. "Supper is just

about done, so why doesn't everybody take a seat in the dining room and I'll start to bring things in?"

"Can I help with anything?" Madison asked.

"That's all right," Victoria said, slicing up the bread and putting the knife back inside the drawer. "You and Tom go sit down."

Mason stood in the doorway to the dining room, bowing slightly to them as they passed. "After you," he said, motioning them toward the table.

"Hope you like chicken," Victoria said, placing the platter on the table.

"Chicken's great," Madison said, standing behind her seat. "Are you sure I can't help you?" she asked again.

"No thank you," Victoria replied with a tight grin. She retreated back into the kitchen and Mason followed her.

"She said she didn't need help!" Tom called after his father, but he was shrugged off.

"Sit down," Tom said, pulling out one of the chairs. He parked himself in the one next to hers. After a moment Tom's parents returned with the rest of the dishes.

"I think that's it," Victoria said.

Mason picked up a bottle of wine from the center of the table.

"I'd offer you guys some wine, but I'm not sure how your aunt and uncle would feel about me giving you alcohol," he said, inserting the corkscrew into the top of the bottle. "And besides, Tom can't drink because of his condition."

Tom shot his father a look that could have peeled paint from the wall.

"Mason." Tom's mother shook her head sadly.

"What did I say?" he asked, looking around the room for someone to answer. "I assumed she knew," he said, the cork coming free of the bottle with a loud pop.

"I do know," Madison said, nodding, a polite smile on her face.

Tom was about to say something to his father about being a complete jerk when he felt Madison's hand touch his briefly under the table, and his anger was suddenly diffused. "It's fine," he managed instead.

"All right," his mother said with a sigh of relief. "Shall we eat?"

She picked up the knife and started to carve the chicken.

And from that point things seemed to return to normal, his father keeping his comments to the Red Sox and how the *Farmers' Almanac* had predicted a very wet and humid summer.

"So you're from Chicago," his mother said to Madison, tearing off a corner of bread and popping it into her mouth. "And you'll be visiting just for the summer?"

Madison became noticeably uncomfortable, looking down at her plate. "Probably longer," she mumbled. "I'll probably be going to school here."

Tom gave his mother a nasty look across the table.

"I'm sorry," she said, brushing the crumbs from her hands. "Did I touch on something I shouldn't have?"

"See," his father said, taking a sip from his glass of wine. "It's very easy to do. I do it all the time, it seems."

Madison raised her head and smiled anxiously. "That's all right, Mrs. Lovett," she said. "It's just that my parents are in the process of splitting up and they think it might be best for me to stay with my aunt and uncle for a while."

"I'm sorry, hon," his mother said sympathetically. "I didn't mean to upset you."

Holding his breath, Tom reached down under the table and searched for Madison's hand. His hand landed on her leg instead and he quickly yanked it away.

Madison picked up her water glass and took a drink, turning her head ever so slightly and smiling at him. He almost said he was sorry but decided against it. She didn't appear to be at all upset.

"So, who'd like some dessert?" his mother asked after downing the remainder of her wine. She stood and started to clean up. "I think there's some Ben & Jerry's downstairs in the freezer," she said, reaching for their plates. "Mason, go get the ice cream. We'll make sundaes."

"I'm totally stuffed," Madison said, patting her perfectly flat stomach. "But I think I might be able to find room for ice cream."

Tom had suggested that they have their dessert outside, so they took their heaping bowls out to the patio, where they could have some privacy.

They sat in the cool darkness, eating and talking.

"Sorry about my parents," Tom said, stirring the contents of his bowl. "They can be kind of obnoxious."

"Do you mean the stuff about *my* parents? That was fine," she said through a bite of ice cream. "There was no way your mom could have known."

He made a face as he took a bite of his dessert.

"I thought you were gonna freak when your dad mentioned your condition," she said.

"My condition," he said with a certain amount of disgust. "They just love to bring it up whenever they can. It's like they're so aware of it—they feel it's necessary to make sure that everybody else knows about it too." Tom shook his head. " It's like the only thing they have to talk about with anyone," he said with a scowl and an angry shake of his head. Then he got very quiet, pulling his bowl of ice cream closer and picking up his spoon.

"The next time your mom and dad bring it up with

somebody, you should pretend to have an attack and fall on the ground," she said, the words spilling out before she had the chance to put on the brakes.

It's a curse, it really is, Madison thought as she watched Tom's eyes widen at her suggestion. It was as if her brain made it a point to come up with the worst-possible things to say.

But then the corners of Tom's mouth began to quiver and he began to laugh, not just chuckle but really laugh. "That would be pretty funny," he gasped. "I can just see the looks on their faces. This is Tom; he has narcolepsy—wham! Right to the ground."

Madison let herself go, allowing her laughter to bubble up and out of her.

And then she let out a snort.

Her hands immediately went to her face as she covered an embarrassed blush.

"That always happens when I laugh really hard," she said. "It's gross, I know."

He nodded. "I think I'd rather have narcolepsy," he managed before breaking down into hysterics again.

It took them a good five minutes to pull themselves together long enough to finish their ice cream.

"That felt good," Madison said, after a brief moment of silence.

Tom smiled, finishing the last of his dessert. "It did," he agreed, grabbing up his napkin and wiping vigorously at his mouth. "It's been a while since I had something to laugh about."

"How have you been feeling?" she asked, licking her spoon. "You had the bad attack the other day; anything since?"

Something was definitely bothering Tom, something she wasn't sure he wanted to discuss.

"You don't have to talk about it if makes you uncomfortable," she said, ready to change the subject to something lighter.

"It's not that," he said. "I just don't know how to explain it. Something happened last night. I don't think it was an attack, but I couldn't tell you what it was. I just know that it's making me a little nervous."

"How did you feel this morning?" she asked.

"Fine," he answered with a shrug. "Other than the fact that I sorta just knew something wasn't right."

"Do you feel better now?"

"I feel good," he told her, "but it doesn't take away the nagging feeling that something happened. I'm just scared this whole Quentin's narcolepsy thing is getting worse." He laughed nervously. "Man, can I bring a party down or what?" he said. "Let's talk about something else before we both decide to cut our wrists."

Madison reacted without thinking, reaching across the patio table to take hold of his hand.

"You're going to be fine," she told him, giving his hand a firm squeeze. "I just know these things."

"Oh yeah?" he asked, a lopsided grin appearing on his face. "And how can you be so sure?"

"Trust me," she said, returning the smile. She liked this guy, *really* liked him, and just the thought of him being upset made her want to reassure him somehow.

The glass door to the patio suddenly slid back and Tom quickly pulled his hand from hers.

"Hey, Tommy," his dad said from the doorway. "It's getting late. I think it's time to say good night to your company."

Tom blushed red, and Madison watched as a spark of anger ignited in his eyes.

"It's only a little after eight," he said, looking at his watch and then at his father.

"Remember what the doctor said about keeping those routines," his father said firmly. "If you're going to get that workout in before bedtime—"

"Screw the workout," he snapped, angrily slamming his hand down on the table. "This is crap."

"I don't care if you have company or not," Mason Lovett said, coming out of the house onto the patio.

"You do not speak to me in that tone of voice—ever. Do I make myself clear?"

Madison stood up, reaching over to touch Tom's hand. "It's all right," she told him. "I should probably be getting home anyway."

Tom stood as well, his eyes never leaving his father.

"Why does it bother you so much to see me acting like a normal person?" he asked.

"Tom, don't start. I just want you to . . ."

Madison was feeling incredibly uncomfortable and was about to excuse herself from their conversation when she noticed a strange look appear on Tom's face.

And then he went suddenly rigid, his head snapping back violently as he lurched to one side.

"Tom?" she asked, reaching out to him.

"Not . . . now," he said in a whisper, falling backward into the table and then to the ground.

"Oh my God!" she shrieked, dropping to her knees beside him. Madison watched, horrified—helpless—as Tom's eyes slowly began to close. There was such fear in his expression.

"It's going to be okay," she told him, taking his hand in hers. She fought to keep her voice from quavering. "Remember what I said; I know these things."

Mason Lovett came through the doorway and stood beside her.

"Excuse me, Madison," he said, practically pushing her out of the way. "We'll take it from here."

She moved out of his way as Tom's mother ran out onto the deck. The two of them pulled the unconscious boy to his feet and half carried, half dragged him back into the house.

Madison didn't know how long she stood there, expecting at least one of Tom's parents to come out and tell her how he was doing, but nobody came. And after a while, certain that she had been forgotten in all the activity, she climbed the fence back to her aunt and uncle's yard. The vision of Tom falling unconscious flashed again and again before her eyes.

A sight she would never forget.

CHAPTER 9

The eleven o'clock news had already begun, and Madison was still too wound up to call it a night. She had put the television on in her room, hoping that it would lull her to sleep. Hours later, she still couldn't get over the image of Tom Lovett crumpling to the ground.

After a few minutes she gave up, grabbed her pillows, stuffed them behind her back, and opened her journal in her lap.

Her eyes skimmed the entries she had made over the last couple of days and she smiled. Almost every one of them had a reference to Tom. She glanced out the window, biting her lip, and again wondered if he was all right. It didn't matter that they had just met; Tom felt like the one solid thing in her life right then, and all she wanted to think about was spending more time with him.

Jotting down the date and time, Madison began her entry. Her writing had become almost stream of consciousness, unfiltered thoughts and feelings spilling onto the empty page. Tonight she would write about her experience at Tom's house. She was surprised at how much detail she remembered, as if her eyes had been cameras, taking mental pictures of everything she had seen. The first thing she recalled was Tom's smile when he opened the door and how warm it made her feel to think that somebody was actually that happy to see her. She liked that smile. She could definitely get used to seeing it every day.

Madison paused, looking up from her journal at the television. A newswoman with perfectly styled blond hair was reading a story about a local politician arrested for drunk driving and how this was his seventh offense.

Sucks to be you, dude, she thought, going back to writing.

It was odd, but she had noticed that Tom didn't look like either one of his parents. Sure, his dad was sort of tall and thin like Tom and his mom had the same sandy blond hair, but there was usually more of a family resemblance, something that made it obvious they shared the same genes. She had inherited her father's slightly protruding ears and fair skin and her mother's nose. When she was standing side by side with her parents, there was no mistaking whose kid she was. In Tom's case, though, she just didn't see it.

Madison leaned her head back against her pillows and closed her eyes. She was starting to feel tired. Closing her journal, she leaned over to the nightstand and opened the drawer, placing the book inside. She slid the drawer closed and was thinking about brushing her teeth when something on the news broadcast caught her attention—they were saying something about narcolepsy.

Madison crawled down to the foot of the bed, listening to the story. The scene switched from the anchor desk to a film of a lake in Maine. There were boats and divers in the water and the voice-over said that they were searching for a man who had been reported missing by his sister.

Madison was just about to dismiss what she thought she had heard when the missing man's name was read: Quentin.

Isn't that the name of Tom's illness? Quentin's narcolepsy? She was almost sure it was.

She listened more closely.

The story went on to describe Quentin as a Boston native and Harvard Medical School graduate who specialized in narcolepsy and in 1980 had been responsible for the discovery of a rare version of the sleep disorder that bore his name.

Madison was riveted, staring at the television screen as black–and–white photographs of Bernard Quentin were shown—one of them of the smiling man wearing a tuxedo and accepting some sort of award.

The newscaster returned and finished up the story by saying Quentin had been living at his Maine cabin since his retirement in the early spring and had not been heard from since late May, when he had last spoken to his sister. The search of the lake and sur-rounding woods would continue at sunup.

How weird is that? Madison thought, rolling onto her back to look at the ceiling. She made a mental note to be sure to tell Tom all about it, but she won-dered how long it would be this time until she saw him again.

The bed beneath her was beginning to feel incredi-bly comfortable, her eyes growing heavier. She forced herself to roll off the bed and walk over to the television to turn it off. On the way she passed the window and glanced through the sheer curtains at the Lovetts' house next door.

There was a black van parked in the driveway, its engine idling as if waiting for somebody.

Madison turned off the television and then the

lamp, plunging the room into darkness. She padded back to the window.

Who could be over there at this hour? she wondered, standing to the side of the window so she couldn't be seen from the driveway. She checked the van's side to see if there was any writing on it. It was blank, its reflective surface shining in the light that emanated from the Lovetts' house.

At that moment three figures exited the garage, approaching the van very quickly.

What's the rush? she wondered, noticing how they were all dressed in dark clothes. One of the men climbed into the driver's seat while another slid open the side door of the vehicle for the smallest of the three to crawl into the back.

The smallest of the three. *There was something about that one—the way he moved.* She pulled back the curtain for a better look. *Something familiar.*

The light from the driveway caught the side of the third person's face just as he was about to disappear into the belly of the van.

It was Tom Lovett.

There has to be a mistake, she told herself, watching as the second of the three men quickly slid the door closed and climbed in on the passenger side. The van backed down the driveway into the street.

Her heart hammered in her chest as she got in bed and pulled the covers tightly around herself. Who were those men, and why would they be taking Tom out so late and so soon after a narcoleptic attack?

Madison had felt like something was up with Tom, more than what he or his family admitted, but now it was becoming clear. Tom and his parents were most definitely involved in something, and Madison had the feeling it wasn't anything good.

The trap had been set, and all Tremain had to do was sit back and wait for it to be sprung.

He sat at a small circular table wedged into the motel room's corner, its wooden surface mottled with years of burns and deep gouges. An unopened pack of cigarettes lay at the table's center, and it took all the strength that he could muster not to tear it open and light one up, followed by a second and likely a third.

This was at least the sixth time he'd done this since deciding to quit, and he wasn't entirely sure why he had. Maybe it was a challenge, he guessed, to see if he was strong enough to overcome the temptation. If he could manage that, then he would be strong enough to deal with just about anything life could throw at him.

And life had been tossing some pretty wild stuff his way lately.

He had taken the job with Pandora for all the right reasons. Tremain wanted to see the world remain safe, but in recent years he had come to realize the world contained a lot more danger than he ever could fathom.

He reached across the table, taking hold of the cigarette package, admiring the red-and-white box more closely. His hands still shook and his thoughts were jumbled, unfocused. God, he missed them, the alcohol, the smokes, one right after another. He was beginning to believe that his thoughts might actually have been clearer then—his brain so sharp that everything had come to him in a flash, that there wasn't a problem he couldn't have easily dealt with.

Despite his best efforts, certain technologies and scientific breakthroughs were finding their way onto the black market. At first it had been chalked up to pure luck and the tenacity of the enemy, but something hadn't seemed right. So he had decided to perform his own, private investigation.

Tremain hadn't liked what he'd found.

His tremulous fingers held the cardboard package, ready to tear the cellophane away to get at the contents, to regain his clarity of thought. But he knew that was a lie: it was the addiction talking. There would be no solution from lungs clogged with smoke, a mind dulled by booze; in fact, it would likely get him killed.

But the temptation was still there.

He placed the still-unopened pack back at the center of the table, suddenly feeling a bit stronger. He glanced at his watch, startled at how quickly the night had passed while he had waited for what, he really wasn't sure. Rising to his feet, he walked around the room, stopping to stretch his arms above his head. He considered lying down, eyeing his bed longingly, but the sun would be rising in a couple of hours, and he could drive to the Tri-State Airport early and take his chartered plane back to Washington.

Instead he decided to take a shower, change into some clean clothes, and be on his way. A part of him was disappointed that nothing had happened during the night. He had thought for sure that ruffling the feathers of Brandon Kavanagh would produce some result to confirm his suspicions. Weeks ago he had been contacted by a scientist on the Janus Project who feared that his advancements were being abused, a scientist who had since gone missing. That plus the intelligence report from Albania had convinced Tremain that Brandon Kavanagh had turned traitor, selling the fruits of Janus to the highest bidder. He had believed that his arrival in West Virginia, and the announcement that Janus was to be shut down, would stir Kavanagh to action against him. But so far, nothing.

Removing his watch, he placed it on the dresser outside the bathroom and started to unbutton his shirt, untucking it from his pants.

Tremain stopped suddenly; he turned and crossed the room, snatching up the cigarettes from the table. He would only have one, and that would be that. *No booze, just one lousy cigarette—a reward for being so damn ambitious*, he thought, heading to the door. He would smoke it outside on the walkway that circled the Twilight Motor Lodge; it was a nonsmoking room, after all.

Tremain eagerly pulled the red piece of stripping from the cigarette packaging, letting the thin plastic drift to the floor of the room. He'd pick it up later.

He undid the locks and threw open the door, allowing the humid West Virginia night to envelop him like a wet blanket. He didn't even notice the boy standing in front of the door until it was too late.

"Hey," the stranger said, a hint of a smile on his all-American features. "I was just about to knock."

Alarm bells went off in his head at the sight of the youth. There was a loaded nine-millimeter Glock pistol hidden beneath the left-side pillow on the bed, and he considered diving for it but never got the chance.

The boy's movement was a blur, one of his legs coming up to kick Tremain in his chest with the flat of his foot, sending him hurtling backward into the room.

Tremain bounced off the wall, falling to all fours, gasping as he tried to suck the oxygen back into his lungs so that he could speak. It was like being underwater: no matter how hard he tried, the air would not come. A shiver of icy cold ran up his spine as he watched the kid quietly pushing the door closed behind him.

"Hope you don't mind," the boy said, the casual smile still on his face.

Instincts honed by years of fieldwork suddenly kicked into overdrive, and he struggled to his feet and dove toward the bed, hoping to reach the pistol hidden beneath the pillow before it was too late.

Everything moved in slow motion. Tremain leapt for the bed, landing on the mattress as his hand slipped beneath the pillow to feel the comforting grip of the Glock. He rolled from the bed in one movement, aiming the weapon at where he imagined his opponent to be.

But the boy was closer than that, and Tremain again marveled at his uncanny speed. He extended his arm, aiming the Glock, desperate to get off at least one shot to slow the boy down before he was upon him. The kid leapt up into the air, spinning completely around, the heel of his shoe connecting with Tremain's gun.

The Glock flew out of Tremain's hand to become embedded in the cheap plaster wall to his left, followed by an angry cry came from the guests in the room next door. The would-be killer pounced, an animalistic viciousness glinting in his eyes, and Tremain could have sworn he heard a growl from someplace deep inside the teen.

It was the first time he had actually seen what Brandon Kavanagh had worked for years to perfect in the flesh, and he hoped he stayed alive long enough to make sure the world never saw it again. *How could they have done this to a child?*

The young man fell on him, driving him back against the bedside table and then to the floor. Tremain looked up into the kid's blue eyes, searching for some sign of humanity, but found only a cold cruelty radiating back at him. It was like looking into a doll's eyes.

This was a killing machine, something set loose upon the world with one purpose and one purpose only. Tremain had only seconds left to act before that purpose would be achieved.

Before he disappeared, the scientist had given Tremain the only weapon that would work at a time like this, a single word that would shut the murder machine down as if a switch had been thrown. And as the killer wrapped his hands around Tremain's throat, he greedily sucked air into his lungs and was able to speak that word.

"Janus."

The young assassin's eyes widened. For a second he was completely still, frozen. Then he reared back, clutching his head as if it were about to explode, and fell motionless to the floor.

As if one word had struck him dead.

Madison couldn't stand it any longer. Thoughts of last night's strange events haunted her, and she knew the only way to get a grip was to see Tom.

Her brief sleep had been far from restful, filled with bizarre dreams where her friend lay unconscious on his kitchen floor while his parents casually ate their dinner, their food morphing into gigantic ice cream sundaes that looked more like ice sculptures than desserts.

How weird is that?

She grabbed her sweats from the foot of the bed and quickly pulled them on, glancing at the clock to see 4:53 a.m. shining in the murky darkness. She tied up her sneakers and quietly left her bedroom. It was Sunday, and she didn't want to wake Marty and Ellen. Descending the steps to the foyer, Madison went out the front door into the early morning. A light fog drifted over the street, making the usually boring cul-de-sac look sort of creepy.

She crossed the dew-wet grass to the house next door, trying to think of what she would say when they answered the door. *Maybe Tom'll answer,* she thought hopefully, and then, seeing that he was all right, she could go back to bed and sleep peacefully. But her luck didn't usually work that way. *His dad will probably answer,* she imagined as she climbed the steps to the front porch. He looked like an early riser. One of those guys who got up at the crack of dawn just so he could have a cup of coffee and read the newspaper before anybody else. She knew the type well, having lived with one for the last seventeen years.

Madison raised a hand to knock.

What the hell are you doing? an incensed voice inside her head hissed. *It's not even five o'clock in the morning.* She knew the voice was right, but she couldn't think of another way to calm herself down. *You're going to regret this,* the voice of reason scolded as her balled fist rapped three times on the door.

"You're probably right," she mumbled under her breath as she stepped back, folding her arms across her chest, steeling herself.

Nothing happened for what seemed like a very long time, and she was considering knocking again when the porch light went on and she heard the sound of the door being unlocked from the inside. Her pulse quickened, and even though she wasn't really all that religious, she said a silent prayer that it would be Tom on the other side of the door.

Instead a bewildered-looking Mason Lovett stood in the doorway, looking very much as he had last night. He was dressed in the same clothes. He either had a very unimaginative wardrobe or he'd been up all night. Looking at the circles under his eyes and the heavy shadow on his face, she guessed the latter.

"W-what . . . ?" he stammered. "Madison . . . right?"

She nodded.

"What are you doing here?" he asked, with a chuckle that did very little to mask his annoyance. "Is everything all right?"

"I'm worried about Tom—is he okay?" she blurted.

"Madison, it's five o'clock in the morning. Tom is still—" Mason began.

"Is he even here?" Madison interrupted.

The man looked startled. "Of course he's here. He's asleep; why—"

"He didn't have to go to the hospital or anything? I thought I saw him leave last night—in a van. I was worried."

A slight smirk appeared at the corner of Mason

Lovett's mouth. Again she was struck by how little his son resembled him.

"Tom's fine," he said, the smirk turning into a smile. "He recovered from the attack a little while after you left, and then he went straight to bed."

"I saw him get into a van and—"

Tom's father shook his head. "You saw no such thing," he corrected. "Tom went up to bed, and that's where he's been ever since."

"But I saw him," she insisted. There was no way she could have mistaken last night's events.

"You saw wrong," Mason answered firmly. "Tom's been home, in his room, asleep, all night long. Okay?" He was smiling again, clearly urging her to surrender.

"Can I see him?" she asked. "Could you wake him up and tell him that I'd like to talk to him?"

Mason's smile quickly turned to a scowl. "No, I will not wake him up. The boy needs his sleep, and besides, it's five in the morning."

"But I just want to—"

He cut her off before she could plead her case. "Look," he said, stepping back into the house, ready to shut the door. "I need to get ready for work. I'm sure Tom will give you a call when he wakes up."

And before Madison could say another thing,

Mason Lovett had closed the door and the porch light above her head winked out.

She replayed the whole encounter in her head as she returned home, more convinced than ever that she had not imagined last night's events. The odd expression that had appeared on Mason's face when she had mentioned seeing Tom getting into a van nagged at her.

It looked like Tom's father had known exactly what she was talking about.

So then why had he lied?

Tom Lovett came awake with a start, the memory of his latest narcoleptic attack painfully fresh in his mind.

Hoping that he'd only been asleep for a short time, he raised himself up on his elbows and looked around.

"Mom? Dad?" he called out, his eyes taking in his foreign surroundings. "Madison?" An anxious lump formed in his throat; he was desperate for a familiar presence.

He appeared to be in a cabin, sparsely furnished with slip-covered furniture, hardwood floors, and a large stone fireplace, a fire blazing within.

"I . . . I've been here before," Tom said aloud in sudden realization as he climbed to his feet. His eyes caught sight of a large fish—a bass, stuffed and mounted on a plaque hanging above a bookcase crammed with leather-bound books that he'd known would be there. Gradually he was starting to remember this place, but he didn't have the slightest idea why, or how, he had come to be there now.

"Hello, Tom," a voice said behind him, and he whirled around to find a man with a wild head of snow white hair sitting in a wingback chair in the corner, a halo of smoke from the pipe he was puffing on drifting above his head. "I'm sure this all seems a bit odd right now, but if you'll give me a chance . . ."

"You," Tom gasped, horrifying imagery—memories of an old man feeding a fire, then dying violently as his chest was struck with bullets—filling his mind. "In a dream . . . I watched you die."

The old man calmly smoked his pipe. "If you are here with me now, that's probably so," he said sadly. Then his eyes glazed over and he seemed to become lost in thought. "Actually, if you're here with me, then I am most definitely dead." His eyes snapped back into focus and he returned his attention to Tom. "And you were my killer," he stated, pulling the pipe from his mouth and jabbing at him with its stem.

Tom's body tingled with panic. He had to get away from this place—this crazy old man. He had to get home, where it was safe.

"I can't stay here." He headed across the room, knowing where the door would be.

"You don't want to do that, Tom," the old man called out behind him, grunting as he pulled himself up out of the chair. "You're better off here with me, at least for a little while longer."

Tom strode down the hallway with purpose, the hardwood floor creaking beneath his feet. He knew that if he stayed another second, he would lose his mind. He had to get home.

"Tom, don't," the old man pleaded from the end of the hall.

But Tom wasn't listening. He reached out and grabbed the metal doorknob. It was cold to his touch, so cold that it stuck to the flesh of his hand. But that didn't stop him. He threw open the door. And nothing could have prepared him for what awaited him outside the cabin.

Nothing.

Nothing, for as far as his eyes could see, an ocean of darkness spread out before him. He grabbed the door frame to halt his momentum, to keep from being thrown out into the cold void. Then movement in the hallway behind him caught his attention, and he turned away from the universe of black to see the old man watching him.

"You don't want to go out there," he said, slowly raising the pipe to his mouth for another puff. "No up or down, just emptiness. Come back inside where it's more hospitable," the man said kindly. "I won't bite. I'm Dr. Quentin, Bernard Quentin, and the answers to your questions are here with me."

"So you're telling me that this isn't real?" Tom's voice was tinged with skepticism. He sat on the ancient sofa in the cabin, a spring somewhere beneath the threadbare cushion poking him uncomfortably in the butt.

"It's called a mental construct," Quentin said from his seat across the room. He tapped the side of his head with a finger. "A calm place inside your mind. I based it on my cabin in Maine. I used to bring in pictures to show you. You always asked when you could visit—you said that it looked so peaceful you wished you could live there."

The old man chuckled as he tapped the contents of his pipe out into an ashtray resting on a small table beside his chair.

Tom felt sick to his stomach but didn't know how that was possible, since this was all supposedly happening inside his head.

"But I don't know you." He shook his head vigorously. "The first time I ever saw you was in a dream where . . ." His voice trailed off, the terrifying images of the nightmarish hallucination again flashing in rapid fire across his mind's eye.

"Where I was murdered?" Quentin finished casually. He stuck his finger inside the bowl of his pipe and scraped out the last of the blackened tobacco. "It's quite all right, really," the old man offered. "It was something I always suspected would happen. And actually, it needed to happen so that you could find your way here."

"So you're not real either—you're a, what did you call it? A mental construct?"

Quentin smiled and nodded. "Yes, a mental construct based on a memory. Part of an interactive program downloaded directly into your brain. Amazing, isn't it? It's almost as if I'm still alive."

Tom felt like he was about to jump out of his skin. This was insane, and he had no doubt that his narcoleptic condition was somehow responsible. *Is it possible for narcolepsy to mutate into insanity?*

"Dr. Quentin, I don't know you," he said, sliding forward on the most uncomfortable couch a psychotic mind could conjure. "I mean, I know *who* you are because of my condition and all, but I've never met you—you're just a name, somebody that my screwed-up illness is named after."

The old man had removed a tobacco pouch,

wedged into the side of his seat cushion, and was refilling his pipe.

"We have met before, Tom," Quentin assured him, packing the tobacco tightly into the bowl. "It's just that you don't remember. That's the way it is with the project."

Tom buried his face in his hands. "I wish I could wake up," he moaned under his breath, but he knew that the strange, hallucinogenic dream would have to run its course first.

Raising his face from his hands, he looked at the old man. "Fine, I'll play along. Who or what is the project? Aliens, maybe—I've never hallucinated them before."

The doctor struck a match and lit his pipe. "I can only imagine how overwhelming this must be for you," he said, drawing on the stem, igniting the contents of the bowl. Plumes of sweet-smelling tobacco billowed from the man's mouth as he extinguished the burning match and tossed it into the ashtray. "The project is the Janus Project, and it has made you what you are today."

Tom shuddered as a sudden chill ran up and down his spine. "Made me into . . . ? Into what? I don't understand."

Quentin quickly raised a hand. "Everything will be clear in time, but first we must start at the beginning, and that, I'm afraid, is with me." The doctor's expression grew very grim and his eyes became glassy as he seemed to gaze right through Tom.

"It was all an accident, really," he said dreamily. "I had never intended for my research to be used in such a way, but I would have done just about anything to help Michael."

"Michael?" Tom interrupted. "Who's Michael?"

The doctor smiled sadly. "Michael was my son," he explained. "And my sole reason for beginning to research narcolepsy."

"Your son had it?"

The doctor nodded. "And it wasn't your normal, run-of-the-mill form of the sleep disorder either. It was something much larger—much more incapacitating."

"Quentin's narcolepsy," Tom whispered.

"The very first patient to be branded with that moniker," the doctor added, gazing out into the past. "His case was quite severe, and it seemed to grow worse as he matured." He sighed, setting his pipe down in the ashtray. "I did everything I could to find a way to make him well. We performed every type of physical test imaginable and then performed them again, just to be certain we hadn't missed anything. But we still learned practically nothing, and Michael's condition continued to worsen."

Tom looked around the room as the man spoke, his

eyes falling on a framed picture resting on the mantel above the fireplace. "Is that him?" he asked, walking over to the photograph.

Michael was sitting on a bed, surrounded by books, smiling weakly. He was good looking, with brown hair, and when Tom looked closely, he could see the resemblance to the doctor.

"It wasn't long after that picture was taken that he . . ." Quentin's words seemed to become stuck in his throat, and Tom looked over to see that the old man was overcome with emotion.

"What happened to him, Doctor?" Tom asked, fearing the answer but needing to know.

"I was so wrapped up in my research that I didn't noticed how withdrawn he'd become, how depressed." His voice was filled with pain, as if each and every syllable were razor sharp, cutting as they left his mouth. "My son took his own life one October morning, using the very medications that I had prescribed to help him."

The old man seemed to become smaller, bowing his head in sadness as he sank deeper into the embrace of the wingback chair.

Tom set the picture back on the mantel and quietly returned to the couch.

Quentin slowly regained his composure. "I became

lost in my grief, throwing myself deeper into my research, hoping to find a way to help so that others would not suffer as my Michael had."

The doctor paused.

"And that was when Brandon Kavanagh walked into my life."

With the mention of the man's name, Tom's body suddenly felt like it had been thrown under a cold shower, the gooseflesh rising on the skin of his arms, the hair at the back of his neck standing on end. But as far as he could recall, he had never heard the name until now.

"I'm sure you don't remember him," Quentin said with a vague shake of his head. "And for that I truly envy you."

Tom rubbed his arms to warm them up as he waited for Quentin to explain.

"Kavanagh worked for the government," he said, chewing on the end of his pipe. "He was in charge of a highly classified project that at the time I knew nothing about. All I knew was that he had seen my research on Quentin's narcolepsy and believed that somehow the sleep disorder that had caused the death of my son could provide the missing piece of a puzzle that had managed to evade him for years."

"And this was the Janus Project?" Tom asked.

"Exactly," Quentin answered. "The Janus Project had been attempting to artificially create a form of multiple personality disorder where two distinct personas would exist in one body."

"Why would somebody want that? What would the benefit be to making somebody mentally ill?"

"That's why there are people like Brandon Kavanagh in the world," Quentin responded. "He believed that this was the way to create the ultimate assassin: a compassionate, rational thinking being one moment and then, with the flick of a switch, a conscienceless killing machine that would stop at nothing to complete its mission."

"I still don't see what your research into narcolepsy had to do with creating assassins," Tom argued, unsure why Quentin was telling him all this; not that his hallucinations ever really had to make sense.

Quentin sat with his eyes closed and gripped the arms of the chair as if bracing himself for something painful to come. "Kavanagh had seen something in my research—the missing component, something in the chemical makeup of my patients' brains—that would make them susceptible to the process Janus had developed to fragment the personalities of test subjects."

"What good is a narcoleptic assassin?" Tom asked.

"Only one of the personalities would have the

sleeping disorder, to be used as a kind of fail-safe if necessary," Quentin said, slowly opening his eyes.

Tom stared at the old man, the truth finally dawning on him.

"A microchip was surgically implanted in the subject's brain. When activated, it would stimulate a narcoleptic seizure, acting as a kind of switch, turning off the existing personality and allowing the artificially created persona to become active."

"Why are you telling me this?" Tom asked, an edge of panic in his voice. An area of his scalp had suddenly become quite itchy, but he ignored the discomfort, totally engrossed in the old man's words.

Quentin focused on the boy. "You have to know—before it's too late, before any more damage is done."

Tom suddenly laughed nervously, getting up from the couch to pace around the room. "This is nuts," he said, digging deeply into his memories for any exercise that might free him from this most disturbing of hypnagogic hallucinations.

"The most susceptible to the conditioning are children," the doctor continued, a tremble in his voice. "I imagine it has something to do with brain development, but they take to the process much more effectively than the adult subjects."

Quentin laughed sadly, that faraway look again

appearing in his weary eyes. "Kavanagh was so excited that he scoured the world's orphanages, searching for unwanted children born with the symptoms of Quentin's narcolepsy. He called them his special babies—I was surprised by how many he was able to find."

The headache came on him in an instant, a sharp, throbbing pain deep inside his skull that pulsed excruciatingly with the beat of his heart. Tom groaned as he placed his fingertips to his temples. "You did . . . you did experiments on kids?"

"He said that he was giving them a purpose—a chance they would never have had if it wasn't for him." Quentin shook his head slowly. "He truly believed that we were doing a good thing."

The agony inside Tom's head was growing worse, and he was finding it difficult to keep his balance. "What's happening to me?" he asked, his voice beginning to slur. He stumbled backward against the mantel.

Ignoring Tom's question, Quentin went on. "I was a fool, completely blind to the insanity that I'd become a part of. By the time I truly realized what he was doing, it was too late."

The room started to spin, and the pressure inside his skull continued to build. "I'm going to be sick," Tom gasped, pushing off from the fireplace and lurching across the room. The floor seemed to move beneath his feet, as if this dream world was starting to warp, to break apart.

Quentin's voice was low, ashamed. "We took children and hid monsters inside them."

The throbbing inside Tom's head was so severe, he almost wished that he would die just to make it stop. He had to get away. He would rather risk the unknown of the darkness outside than stay in this cabin a moment longer. He staggered toward the front door. The bizarre dream cabin started to tremble violently.

But Quentin reached out, grabbing his arm in a steely grip, preventing his escape from the disintegrating dream place. "We don't have much time left, and there's still so much to tell you." There was panic in the doctor's voice.

Tom tried to pull his arm free, but the doctor held fast. "Let me go," he demanded. The walls of the cabin creaked and moaned, bending impossibly, as if made of rubber. "I can't stand it anymore. . . . I have to wake up."

"Listen to me, Tom," Quentin bellowed over the noise. "The children of Janus were supposed to be the perfect weapons—weapons that had no idea they were weapons. Do you know why I'm telling you this, Tom?"

The cabin lurched to one side, loosening Quentin's grip on his arm, and Tom managed to pull away. "I can't listen to this anymore," he cried, starting down the shifting corridor in a spastic run.

The cabin door loomed ahead of him and he reached for it, just as something began to pound savagely on the other side. Tom froze, watching as the wood of the door trembled and shook from the force of the blows.

He turned and saw that Dr. Quentin stood at the end of the hallway, smoking his pipe. "What is it?" Tom asked.

"The truth," Quentin said, puffing on his pipe, creating a swirling fog that threatened to envelop him. "The truth is on the other side of that door."

The smoke grew thicker, spreading down the hallway toward Tom. He felt a sudden warmth on his face and reached up to his nose. His hand came away covered in blood. The door shook in its frame, and he turned back to it. *It has to end now,* Tom thought as he took hold of the numbingly cold knob and flung the door wide.

Tom wanted to scream, but his voice had been taken away. Standing in the darkness outside the door was someone who looked exactly like him, was even dressed like him . . . but something was different. Something about this person was deeply disturbing.

"Hey there, bro," said the doppelganger with an unnerving grin. A dark trickle of crimson flowed from one nostril down his face. "How's it hangin'?"

Tom came out of the hallucination with a violent start, feeling like he'd been hit in the stomach with a sledgehammer. He struggled to catch his breath, gasping for air as he fought his way back to full consciousness. He felt bad, really bad.

That was definitely the worst one ever, he thought. The hypnagogic episode he had just gone through was more awful than the ones where he'd been chased by wolves or had fallen from the roof of a skyscraper, and the one when he'd been buried alive. They'd all seemed terrifyingly real, but this one . . .

He was lying in the fetal position. Suddenly he came to the realization that he wasn't in his bed, the comforting place where he usually came to after his attacks. He seemed to be on the floor someplace, coarse carpeting beneath him. Slowly he uncurled, muscles aching, the dull throb behind his eyes a distant reminder of the excruciating headache he had experienced within his hallucination. He stood carefully, looking around, but everywhere he looked brought only confusion, and he started to panic. *Am I still hallucinating?*

And then he realized that he wasn't alone.

Tom yelped at the sight of a gray-haired man dressed in a T-shirt and slacks standing nearby, pointing a gun directly at his head.

It was a Glock nine millimeter, and how he knew that only added to his anxiety.

A million and one things raced through his mind as he looked around the room, desperate for a rational explanation, almost hoping that this really was another trick of his illness. Tom closed his hands into fists, sinking his fingernails into the soft flesh of his palms, and squeezed, hoping that the pain might break this latest attack, if this was indeed a hallucination.

"There's no need to be afraid," the man said, although he continued to train his weapon on the boy. "My name is Christian Tremain." His voice was rough and gravelly. "I work for a special division of the government. I'm sure this is all a bit overwhelming, but we want to help you."

First the old man working for some freaky group of mad scientists and now this, Tom thought as he backed up into the wall. "Help me wake up, then."

Tremain lowered his weapon. "This isn't a dream,

boy," he said. "You're very much awake and in great danger."

Tom wanted to laugh, it was all so crazy. He decided that he preferred the daymares where he floated off into space or turned into smoke and blew away on the wind.

"I just want to wake up," he whispered, banging his head against the wall behind him with a hollow thunk.

"What's your name, son?" the man asked quietly.

The name Tyler Garrett popped into his head, and for a moment Tom actually forgot his own.

"Tom Lovett," he yelled, forcing the words from his mouth before he could forget again. "My name is Tom Lovett."

"Easy, Tom." Tremain raised a hand in a calming gesture. "I know how crazy this must seem to you, but I do want to help you get through this. The first thing that you have to realize, though, is that this is real—you are not dreaming."

Tom's legs began to tremble, the truth of the man's words slowly sinking in. "How can it be real?" he said, more to himself than to anyone else. "How is this even possible?" He was holding on by a hair; in a matter of moments he was sure he would be screaming.

Tremain moved closer and Tom recoiled, sliding

down the wall, suddenly feeling like a puppet whose strings had been cut.

"Who are you . . . ? What's happening to me? I have to call my parents. . . . I have to—"

"Calm down, Tom," Tremain ordered in an authoritative voice. "Remember what Dr. Quentin told you."

Tom tried to shrink farther into the wall. "How could you know about that?"

"He told me what he was going to do," the man explained. "He told me about the memory implant and how he was going to try to override your programming."

"The Janus Project," Tom whispered. "You know about the Janus Project, but it's just a dream—a hallucination, wasn't it?"

"Tom, you are a result of the science developed by Janus—a science that was supposed to be used for the good of the country but has been subverted by the project's director, Brandon Kavanagh."

"It's finally happened." Tom moaned, burying his face in his hands. "I've finally lost it."

Tremain squatted down in front of him, but Tom no longer had the strength to move away. "You're not crazy," he reassured the youth, reaching out to grab his knee in an encouraging grip. "It's the situation that's crazy."

Tom looked up and gazed into Tremain's steel gray

eyes. After a moment he asked, "Where am I . . . ? Why am I here?"

"You're in a motel in West Virginia," Tremain explained carefully. "You've been sent by Brandon Kavanagh to kill me."

Tom just stared at the man. "Kill you?" he asked, voice raised in panic. A surge of adrenaline coursed through his body as he fought to climb up from the floor. "That's impossible; I would never . . . could never even think of doing anything like that."

Tremain stood as well, the joints in his knees clicking noisily as he straightened. "Check your pockets, Tom. You'll find proof that what I'm saying is true."

Tom took the man's words as a challenge, plunging his hands into the pockets of his black windbreaker. His fingers brushed against two items, one in each pocket, and slowly he removed them.

One was a gun—a Smith & Wesson P99, ten shots fired and one in the clip. The other was a syringe filled with a clear liquid that Tom seemed to know was the concentrated venom of the sea wasp, *Chironex fleckeri*, an extremely poisonous form of jellyfish found only in the waters of Australia. *How do I know this?* he wondered, staring dumbly at the objects.

"These . . . these aren't mine." He shook his head

vigorously, offering the items up to the man standing across from him. "I have no idea how . . ."

"Not yours directly," Tremain said. "But your other half. They were to be used to take my life."

Tom dropped the gun and syringe to the floor, stepping back from them as if they had the ability to attack on their own.

"I can't take this," he said, turning around, looking for a way out of the room. "I have to get out of here. . . ."

"Listen to me, Tom," Tremain said, coming after him. "Dr. Quentin believed that Brandon Kavanagh was planning to sell the technology developed at Janus to the highest bidder and contacted me in an attempt to stop him. Both he and I believed that the only way to stop Kavanagh was to turn the Janus technology against him."

Tom reached the door, yanking it open only to have it stop short as the slide chain reached its limit.

"A process has been started inside your brain, Tom," the man went on. "Unification—where the two halves of your fragmented personality will attempt to merge together to heal as one."

A mirror image of himself—a bad version, from his hallucination, standing behind the door of Quentin's cabin—filled his brain.

"Hey there, bro. How's it hangin'?"

"We can help you, Tom," Tremain said behind him. "And you can help us."

The man's hand closed around Tom's upper arm and Tom reacted, taking hold of Tremain's wrist, twisting it effortlessly to one side and driving him painfully to his knees. Instinctively Tom knew he could break the man's wrist at that moment but decided against it.

"Don't touch me," he said, speaking in a voice that wasn't entirely his own. "Don't you ever touch me."

He kicked the man away and turned, pulling the chain from the track and throwing open the door, running for the stairs that would take him to the parking lot below. He had never been here before, but somehow he knew how to get away, and he let the strange intuition guide him.

Tom moved through the darkness as if it were second nature, as if he had been doing this his entire life. Something told him to work his way toward the entrance to the driveway, and he did so, darting across the expanse of parking lot to the base of an illuminated signpost. He peered at the dark road beyond and realized he didn't have the slightest clue where to go next. He was on his own, the strange force that had been guiding him suddenly absent.

Immediately he thought of his parents and looked across the lot at the Starlight Motel's main office.

"I'll ask if I can use their phone and—" he muttered to himself.

The screeching of brakes and the roar of an engine interrupted his plans as a black van turned off the main road and barreled up the drive. Tom stepped back, nearly tripping over the concrete base of the signpost as the vehicle came to an abrupt stop in front of him. The side door of the van slid open to reveal a man dressed entirely in black, a man who seemed to know him.

"What the hell happened to you?" the man from the van asked in an angry whisper. "Why weren't you at the rendezvous point?"

Tom's mouth moved to answer, but the words wouldn't come. He had no idea how to respond.

"Sleeper One?" the man asked, jumping out of the vehicle, eyeing him with caution. "Are you all right? Everything finished here?"

"I—I . . ." Tom stammered. "I don't know what you're talking about. . . ."

"What's the problem, Crenshaw?" a voice asked impatiently from the driver's seat of the van.

"Think we have a little identity crisis here," Crenshaw responded, his hand going to an object concealed in a leather holster attached to his belt.

Tom didn't have a clue what the man was reaching

for, assuming at first that it was a gun but then remembering that all transport agents carried Tasers.

Transport agents? It was as if he were thinking with somebody else's brain. And what the hell was a Taser?

"Deal with it and let's go," the driver ordered.

Crenshaw pointed the Taser at Tom, and he was temporarily mesmerized by the blinking green light on top of the device. But then his senses started to scream that he was in danger.

Tom was on the move before he realized what he was doing. Listening to the shrieking instincts inside his skull, Tom broke into a run. Crenshaw took off after him. As Tom dove toward a patch of shadow behind the signpost, he was startled by a high-pitched whine, and a burning pain shot through his side. Tom froze and glanced down at two projectiles lodged in his side; they were attached to thin, coiled wires leading back to the device in Crenshaw's hand.

"Lights out," Tom heard the man say as fifty thousand volts of electric current passed through his body, overriding his central nervous system.

Fighting to stay conscious, Tom felt himself hauled up from where he had fallen and then dumped unceremoniously into the belly of the waiting van.

"We'll get him back to his handlers and they can

worry about what to do from there," he heard Crenshaw say from someplace very far away.

"Sounds like a plan," the driver responded. "The sooner he's somebody else's responsibility, the better."

As Tom spiraled deeper into oblivion, he heard Crenshaw laugh and felt the van begin to move. "What's the matter, Burt?" the man asked his partner. "Sleeper One a little too much for you?"

"Let's just say I'd be more comfortable driving nuclear ordnance," Burt responded.

"The kid gives me the creeps," were the last words Tom heard before slipping down into a very dark place.

It was like something out of one of those black-and-white horror movies that Tom and his dad rented around Halloween. He stood on the front steps of an old, run-down mansion with those two questions he seemed to be asking himself a lot lately. *Where am I, and how did I get here?*

Everything came back to him in a rush, and it just about knocked him on his back. He remembered it all— the dream conversation with Dr. Quentin, his nasty twin on the other side of the cabin door, waking up in the motel room—*At least, I think I woke up.* It was getting harder to tell the difference between reality and hallucination.

And then he remembered the van, and he unconsciously rubbed at his side. *Was that real or another trick of my sick—and obviously getting sicker—mind?* He really didn't know for sure.

So, where now? Tom thought anxiously, stepping back down the rickety wooden steps to get a better look at his surroundings.

The front facade of the sprawling mansion was covered in snaking, leafy vines that just about obscured the large front windows of the multifloored structure. He turned around, looking down a stone path overgrown with weeds that wandered into a wall of swirling fog so thick he couldn't see anything beyond it. It was strangely quiet here: no traffic in the distance, no sounds from the house, as if the whole area were encased in a bubble of silence.

"Okay, so this can't be real," Tom decided aloud, trying to calm his increasing panic.

But there was something strangely familiar about this creepy place. He remembered Dr. Quentin's cabin and his explanation of mental constructs. *Maybe that's what this was,* Tom thought, turning back to the mansion's front steps.

Tom started to climb, the old, warped wood beneath his feet creaking with each footfall. At the top of the stairs was a set of large double doors the color of dried blood, paint peeling as if the doors were shedding their skin. As his foot landed on the last step, one of the red doors slowly squeaked open, revealing a grand but dilapidated entryway within. He stopped dead in his tracks, half expecting to see a ghostly white hand beckoning from the shadows. Instead there was a voice.

"Are you going to stand out there with your thumb up your ass all day or are you coming in?"

The voice was familiar. "How do I know it's safe?" he questioned, peering into the entrance, searching for its owner.

He heard a dry chuckle, like the sound of metal ball bearings rolled across a wooden floor. "We're beyond that now, bro," the voice replied, and Tom caught the hint of a southern drawl. "Safe is something we're going to have to work real hard at, so I suggest you get yourself in here right quick so we can get down to business."

This is so friggin' weird, Tom thought as he walked across the porch to the open door. He told himself it was just a hallucination; there was no point in being afraid.

The foyer was just as run down and dilapidated as the front of the building—the floor covered in dried seasonal leaves, dust and dirt. Tom jumped as the door slammed shut behind him.

"Hello?" he called out, his voice echoing under the cathedral ceiling.

Getting no answer, he carefully looked around, up

the winding grand staircase that led to the second floor, straight ahead at a doorway partially enshrouded with a heavy, moth-eaten curtain, to the left at a hallway that went off into the darkness, and to the right into a parlor with its furniture still in place.

Outside, the wind had picked up, and the mansion seemed to moan like somebody in pain. Tom was again reminded of late Saturday nights, sitting beneath a blanket with his dad, bowl of popcorn in his lap, watching some scary movie on television. He wanted to be back there again, with his father—his family. He wanted to be free of what seemed to be a nightmare that just didn't want to quit.

"You felt safe with him, didn't you?" the voice with the southern accent asked.

Tom turned to the darkened parlor.

"Your dad," came the voice again. "He made you feel safe, all nice and secure."

"How do you know I was thinking about my father?" Tom asked as he entered the parlor, eyes squinting, attempting to pierce the murky shadows.

The voice chuckled, and Tom felt an icy finger of dread run up and down his spine. There wasn't even the slightest hint of humor in it; it was more growl than laugh.

A table lamp clicked on, dispelling the inky darkness

from the corner of the room to reveal Tom's twin seated in a high-backed leather chair not two feet from Tom, his hand still on the lamp's pull chain.

"Hey there," he said with a smile.

They were exactly identical, the only difference being that this version of himself wasn't wearing any glasses, and there was something about the expression on his face—the smile. It was cold, more of a sneer than an expression of pleasure, and Tom knew that this young man—this version of himself—was capable of just about anything, no matter how horrible.

"Come on over; take a seat." His twin gestured toward a chair directly across from him. "We got loads to talk about."

Tom clumsily made his way to the proffered chair, eyes never leaving his double as he slowly lowered himself into it. "What exactly are you . . . are you me?" he asked.

His twin laughed again, that same horrible hacking sound. "No, bud, I ain't you," he said, leaning back and casually crossing his legs. "And you sure as hell ain't me."

A name popped into Tom's head as it had done in that West Virginia motel room—the name that had almost made him forget his own. "You're Tyler Garrett."

His double nodded. "I certainly am, and you're Tommy Lovett—the guy who shares my body."

Tom stiffened. "*Your* body?"

Garrett's hands rose to placate. "Okay, okay—*our* body."

The wind wailed fitfully outside. "This is too much." Tom shook his head as he leaned back in his chair. "It's just too friggin' much."

"My sentiments exactly," Garrett agreed. "And the question is, What are we gonna do about it?"

Tom swallowed hard and closed his eyes. "I'm going to wake up and then I'm going to make an appointment to see my doctor and—"

"And they'll have you exactly where they want you," Garrett finished for him.

Tom opened his eyes to stare at Garrett.

"That's right, you'll go and see . . . what's his name?" Garrett asked. "Powell? I know him as Dr. Goyer, but even that probably ain't his real name. Anyway, you'll tell him about your strange dreams and how there's this fella living inside your head who looks just like you only he talks with a good ole boy drawl, and they'll tell you that they have just the thing to make you better."

Tom felt his entire body begin to tremble, and he grabbed hold of the chair's arms to steady himself.

"But what they'll really do is give you a shot to make you all docile and such and bring you back to the homestead—our real home away from home, the place where you and I were created. They'll ship you back to the Janus Project and they'll just wipe your brain clean, and then they'll start from scratch, whipping up two more equally fascinating personalities to share the same space."

Tom wanted to scream, but he remained perfectly still, letting the nightmare wash over him. Biding his time until it was finally over.

"It's going to be different once you wake up," Garrett said, seeming to pluck the thoughts from Tom's mind. "You're not supposed to be the surface personality right now. I am. But our good friends Quentin and Tremain put some kind of fail-safe inside our head that's made us aware of each other's existence—and so here we are."

Garrett reached out to swat Tom's leg. "Trust me," he said with a wink. "I'm just as confused as you are, but I'm better equipped to deal with it on account of my work."

"Your work? You're a killer!" Tom screamed. "A murderer!"

"I'm an assassin and damn good at it too," Garrett corrected sharply. "*Killer* is such an ugly word."

Tom closed his eyes again. He thought of his parents, of Madison, desperately willing himself to wake up.

"It's not gonna work, Tommy," Garrett interrupted. "And they're sure as hell not going to help. No waking up until we deal with the problem at hand."

"And what's that?" Tom asked, tired of all the craziness.

"Hello?" Garrett questioned, standing up and knocking on Tom's skull with a closed fist. "Anybody home? What's the problem? You been paying attention here, boy? We're two distinct personalities living inside one head. Call me crazy, but I think we've got an issue here."

Tom watched his other half drop back into his chair. "So what do you think we should do?" he asked.

Garrett rubbed his chin with a finger, and Tom wondered if that was something *he* did when asked a difficult question.

"My first inclination is to take over completely, to kick your whiny ass to the curb, but something tells me that I wouldn't be able to do it," his double said. "Actually gave it a try once, around the time that you stopped taking your medicine. You had a spell in your doctor's office, got that nasty knot on your head and all." He pointed to his own forehead, smiled, and nodded.

Tom didn't know what to say, staring in horror at his evil reflection.

"Couldn't do it then, probably some kind of built-in deterrent," Tyler explained. "And besides, I kinda doubt that Quentin would allow the person responsible for his murder to take the driver's seat now."

Tom's fear turned to anger and he stood, glaring down at his doppelganger. "I'd never let you take control," he said with a sneer. "I'd fight you."

Garrett shook his head in disgust. "Like you'd have a say. It'd be just like you havin' one of your attacks, only this time I wouldn't be lettin' you back in. But that's neither here nor there," he said, his brow furrowing as he concentrated. "The only way I figure we're both gonna make it out of this alive is if we work together, which is what I think old Doc Quentin might've had in mind."

It was Tom's turn to laugh. "You know what you can do with your offer," he said, walking away, ready to leave the old house and begin his search for a way back to reality, *wherever that was.*

"Don't turn your back on me, boy," Tyler Garrett yelled from the room behind him. "We need each other if we want to live."

Tom ignored him. He threw open the front door and was hit with a blast of wind so powerful that it lifted him from the ground, hurling him across the foyer. He knew it was all part of the hallucination that held him captive, but that did little to squelch the pain he felt in his back as he bounced off the wall opposite the front doors with a sickening thud. He rolled onto his side, splotches of bright orange dancing in front of his eyes as the hurricane-force winds outside the mansion cried like the damned.

"This is my place, Tommy," said a voice very close to his ear, and he pushed himself back against the wall, away from its owner. "I made it myself. My home away from home when you're awake."

Tyler Garrett squatted in front of him, and Tom was strangely fascinated to see *himself* appear so frightening.

"It responds to my feelings," Garrett continued as the winds screamed and moaned, shaking the mansion to its very foundation. "And right now I'm a little upset with you."

He stood, staring down at Tom, who had to shield his eyes from the leaves and airborne grit driven by the wind's onslaught.

"I know you think this is all part of some screwy nightmare, that it's all the creation of your mind, and in a way you're right—but the message is still the same." The double reached down, offering his hand to Tom. "You're not what you think you are," he yelled over the screaming wind. "And if you want to stay alive, you'll take what I'm offering."

Tom stared at the proffered hand hanging in the air before his face.

"They're going to kill you, Tom Lovett," Garrett growled. "They're going to wipe you from existence and me right behind you unless . . ."

Tom wondered if taking Garrett's hand would end this latest creation of his sick mind.

"Well?" Garrett prodded, a halo of leaves swirling around his head.

What do I have to lose? "I want this to be over," Tom screamed over the mournful cries of the elements, reaching out to take hold of Garrett's hand. It was like taking hold of a live wire; his entire body pulsated with an energy that threatened to explode from within him.

"Over?" Garrett scoffed, his flesh beginning to smolder and bubble.

Tom wanted to look away, but he couldn't pull his eyes from the horrible sight as Tyler Garrett began to burn, his flesh blackening as the fire ate away at him.

"We're just getting started, boy," the killer snarled, his voice reduced to a gravelly bark. "We're just getting started."

The ragged words of a killer still echoing in his ears, Tom opened his eyes in the cool semi-darkness. He looked around, searching for some sign that he had at last been freed from the latest bout of ass-kicking, narcolepsy-induced hallucinations.

A consistent droning filled his ears, and a strange airy feeling in the pit of his stomach told him that he definitely wasn't where he wanted to be—at home, in bed, nestled beneath the warmth of his sheets and blankets. Instead a cold metal buckle and a strap fixed him tightly to an uncomfortable seat.

I'm on a plane, he realized as the craft banked sharply to the right, beginning its descent. At first his tired mind wanted to believe that this was just a continuation of the most horrible of daymares, but that same nagging instinct he had felt on awakening in the West Virginia motel room said otherwise. This wasn't a dream at all; this was reality. Whether he liked it or not.

The plane continued its drop as his eyes darted around the compartment, searching for anything that could tell him how and why he'd ended up here. It wasn't a commercial flight he was on but some kind of small transport plane. His hands went to the seat belt, ready to release the buckle and explore the cabin further, but something told him that wouldn't be smart.

The sound of a door sliding open somewhere behind him, followed by voices, told Tom that these new intuitions were probably on the mark.

Tom closed his eyes, pretending to be asleep, listening carefully to the two men drawing closer. He recognized them as the ones from the black van.

Burt and Crenshaw.

"What if he's awake?" the one called Burt was asking.

"Depends on which one is active," Crenshaw replied.

"What do you think went wrong with him?"

"That's for the science geeks back at Janus to figure out. We just worry about transport and delivery."

Tom's heart skipped a beat at the mention of the mysterious project. He could sense them standing very close, watching him as he slept.

"Looks like he's still out," Burt observed. "Hope you didn't do any permanent damage with that thing. Kavanagh'll wear your balls for a hat if you did."

"My balls will be staying right where they are," he heard Crenshaw reply.

Then he felt the man's hand on his wrist, and it took all of his self-control not to scream. *Stay calm,* he told himself. He hoped that he was succeeding in keeping his breathing regular, his heart rate steady.

"Seems fine," Crenshaw told his companion. "Pulse is strong. I think he's just catching up on some beauty sleep."

An intercom crackled to life somewhere in the cabin, and the pilot warned his passengers to prepare for landing. Tom listened as the two men pulled down folding seats from the compartment wall, buckling themselves in just as the plane dropped for its final descent. He wondered where they could possibly be taking him.

He would find out soon enough.

The plane dropped from the sky quickly, tires squealing as they touched down with a violent bounce. They eventually rolled to a stop, the high-pitched whine of the twin engines reduced to a soft hum as the plane powered down.

"This is it," Tom heard Crenshaw say, and then he felt the man's hands at his waist undoing the seat belt. "We'll get him back to his keepers and then we'll be done with him. Give me a hand, will ya?"

"Are you sure he's still asleep?" Burt asked, joining his partner to haul Tom up from his seat.

"He's out like a light, trust me, and if he does wake up, I'll just give 'im another jolt. Relax."

Tom felt himself begin to break out in a cold sweat, remembering the pain of the Taser as it fried his ass into unconsciousness. He didn't want to go through that again.

"Relax, he says," Burt grumbled, throwing Tom's arm around his neck as the two men dragged him toward the exit. "I've heard what this kid can do. It isn't natural."

The men were afraid. He knew that they were talking about him, but it was a side of himself that was still completely unfamiliar. He imagined his double, Tyler Garrett, locked away inside his head. At least, he hoped he was locked away.

The door to the craft opened with a hiss of hydraulics, and a rush of night air flowed into the plane. Tom allowed them to haul him from the craft, the toes of his sneakered feet bouncing off each step as they descended to the runway. He let his head loll limply to one side and through squinted eyes checked out his location. Another black van was parked on the side of the landing field, not far off in a patch of shadow. His kidnappers were bringing him toward it. His head rolled on his shoulders, and as they neared the van, he caught a glimpse of an airport hangar in the distance. He could just about make out the white-painted letters on the side of the corrugated metal structure.

Butler.

Tom couldn't believe it. The decommissioned air force base where he had ridden his bike a few months back. He knew exactly where he was. And he knew what he had to do.

Tom took a deep breath, psyching himself up; then he leapt forward, breaking away from his keepers. Burt screamed in surprise and tried to grab him, but Tom was already running, running faster than he ever had, even though his legs felt like they were made from rubber and would give out on him at any moment.

Just not yet, he begged them, focusing everything he had on getting away. He heard frantic footfalls and the sound of heavy breathing behind him but didn't dare turn around. He knew what he would have seen anyway—Crenshaw coming up fast, nearly breathing down his neck. But then he heard the sound, the now-familiar high-pitched whine of the Taser as it charged up. The man was going to shock him again.

Like hell he is, said a cruel voice inside his skull.

Tom stopped short, spinning around as Crenshaw collided with him. The two stumbled, falling to the ground in a flailing heap. The man was strong, and

Tom knew he couldn't hold out for long. They rolled around, struggled on the pavement.

"Give me a hand!" Crenshaw screamed for his partner.

Tom didn't have a chance against both of them, so he fought harder, trying to break free while avoiding the shocking prongs of the Taser that crackled in his attacker's hand.

Burt was almost there. Tom knew he had to do something.

And then a new force overcame him. He had been aware of it earlier, that strange knowledge of things he had no business knowing about, only this time it was stronger, filling his head with ways to survive.

And Tom listened, suddenly going limp and falling backward to the ground, taking Crenshaw completely by surprise. The man fell forward as Tom brought his head up, smashing the front of his skull into Crenshaw's descending face. There was a snapping sound, and Tom's face was sprayed in a gout of warm blood from the man's broken nose.

He had a nearly overpowering urge to slam the palm of his hand into Crenshaw's face, driving the broken piece of cartilage up into his brain, but Tom pulled back, stifling the violent desire. It was difficult. Something writhing inside him wanted to kill the man, and it took a concentrated effort to hold it back.

He wiggled out from under Crenshaw's moaning form, scrambling to his feet and escaping into the night, running as if the devil himself were hot on his heels.

But he knew the devil wasn't really behind him. *No,* he thought, remembering the cruel voice echoing in his skull.

The devil was much closer than that.

Tom wasn't sure how, but he managed to lose his pursuers, scaling a chain-link fence and throwing himself head-on into the thick underbrush that surrounded the now-closed air force base. His lungs burned as if they were on fire, and his heart beat so rapidly in his chest he worried that it just might burst, but still he ran, sloshing across drainage ditches filled with stagnant, nasty-smelling water and on through densely overgrown sections of Hawthorne wilderness.

He was desperate to find the paths he had taken when he had ridden his bike to the airfield, searching for something—anything—that looked even vaguely familiar. The sound of a truck horn blaring mournfully in the distance spurred him on, and Tom changed direction through the tall grass, moving toward the sound. If he could find his way to the main road—any road, really—he was sure he could get back home.

Home. It was the only place he could think of where he would finally be safe. His parents would know what to do; they would help him.

Something . . . unnatural stirred within his skull at the thought of his family, distracting him, and his foot caught under a root protruding from the moist earth. Tom stumbled forward, fighting to regain his footing, but fell flat on his face. His glasses flew off and the wind was punched from his lungs in a whistling wheeze. For a moment he lay stunned on the damp ground, feeling the moisture from the earth seeping through his light jacket and jeans to chill his flesh.

Disturbing imagery from the evening's experiences poured into his mind, and Tom attempted to break them down into two columns: dream and reality. He was having a difficult time discerning one from the other. If it hadn't all been so frigging scary, he would have laughed himself sick.

Maybe I've just completely lost it, he thought, finally having the common sense to pick himself up from the ground. *Maybe I'm still at home, tucked in bed, trapped inside the mother of all hypnagogic hallucinations.*

He ran his hands along the ground and found his glasses. Rubbing the lenses clean of dirt on his T-shirt, he returned them to his face. He brushed the mud and leaves from his clothes and reexamined his whereabouts.

His pursuers were nowhere to be seen, but that didn't necessarily mean they had given up. The sounds of traffic were closer now, and around him he noticed the remnants of a campfire, complete with empty beer cans and food wrappers. He had to be getting closer to where he wanted to be; he was almost sure of it.

Ahead of him Tom could see an embankment, and he trudged toward it, careful not to repeat his last spill. It wasn't long before he reached the top of the rise and stood looking down into the parking lot of a Li'l Peach convenience store like somebody lost in the desert who had found an oasis. He felt strangely excited as he cautiously descended from the woods into the lot, keeping to the shadows, searching for signs of his captors' shiny black van. *This will all be over soon,* he told himself.

It was still relatively early in the morning, and the store, as well as the road in front of it, wasn't all that busy. Tom had been to this store on his bike trip to explore Butler. He had stopped here to refill one of his tires and buy a bottle of water. And he knew that on the other side of the building, near the air pump, was a pay phone.

Praying that it wasn't out of order, he made his way around the building to the phone, picked up the receiver, and put it to his ear. He leaned heavily against the body of the booth to which the phone was bolted, listening to the sound of the dial tone as if it were the greatest sound he'd ever heard. He called home collect.

His mother picked up on the second ring.

"Mom," he said, hunched over the phone, his mouth close to the receiver. "It's me."

"Tom, where are you? What's going on?" she asked.

He closed his eyes, enjoying the sound of his mother's voice, suddenly very tired and hoping it wasn't a precursor to another attack. In the background he could hear the shuffle of feet across the kitchen floor followed by the muffled sound of his father's voice.

"Tom, where are you?" his mother asked again breathlessly.

"I'm here," he told her, finding it difficult to keep his emotions in check. "Mom, I . . . I think I might be in trouble."

"Trouble? What kind of trouble? Just tell me where you are, Tom, and I'll come and get you right away."

His eyes were burning with emotion, and he suddenly couldn't stand up anymore. He sat down hard on the ground, still clutching the telephone receiver to the side of his face. "There are people chasing me, and I don't know why. Something about me being a killer and—"

"Where are you, Tom?" his mother demanded, and he told her, sobbing now.

"Tom, listen to me." Her voice was calm and soothing. "You stay right where you are. I'm on my way."

His nose was running. *I must look really good,* he thought as he sat under the pay phone, crying like a baby. "I . . . I think I might be going crazy," he managed to get out, his body starting to shake uncontrollably, but not from the cold.

"Calm down, son. Everything is going to be all right," she reassured him.

Tom wanted to believe her. He really did, but he couldn't shake the feeling that it was only going to get worse from here.

CHAPTER 12

Tom held his breath as he watched yet another car turn into the nearly empty Li'l Peach parking lot. Right kind of car, wrong color.

Damn. How long has it been since I called? he wondered, pacing back and forth in front of the pay phone. He considered calling again just to be certain she had left. *What's keeping her?*

A pretty woman with curly blond hair and a flowing, floral print skirt got out of the car, keys in her hand, and hurried into the store. He looked back to the road just as a dark-colored van slowly cruised past. The muscles in his legs tightened, his heart rate increased, the blood pounded in his ears as panic kicked in, and he prepared to run.

But it was a false alarm: the van continued on its way down the road, bypassing the Li'l Peach completely.

As it passed, Tom saw it was dark blue with a white stripe.

Another car pulled into the lot, headlights flashing, and a wave of relief washed over him. His mother, finally. He rushed to meet the metallic green Toyota and was reaching to open the door when sheer panic shot through him in a searing flash. He pulled his hand away as if it had been shoved into fire. He stood before the car, fighting the urge to run.

Opening the driver's side door, his mother emerged. "Tom?" she called to him. "Tom, what's wrong?"

He managed to get control of himself enough to open the car door and get in. "Drive," he ordered, folding his arms across his chest and slouching down.

"What's the matter with you?" his mother asked, getting back in beside him. "You're scaring me."

"I'm sorry," he told her, his voice rising with anxiety. "But just get me out of here. Take me home, please. Please, just drive."

He could feel her eyes on him as she circled the Li'l Peach lot, making her way to the exit on the opposite side. For a while they drove in silence, and as they got closer to home, Tom began to feel slightly better; even the babble of the morning DJs wasn't all that annoying now. He closed his eyes as a song by the Doors began to play and tentatively searched his mind for signs of

Garrett—for the other personality that supposedly shared his brain.

Hello? he thought, imagining an echoing sound in a vast and empty cave. *Anybody there?* There was no answer, but he knew that something was there. Tom recalled the struggle at the airfield and how tough it had been for him not to kill Crenshaw. Something was happening to him. Suddenly he felt very cold.

"I can't keep quiet anymore," his mother blurted, interrupting his thoughts. "I have to know what's going on."

Tom opened his eyes and scrunched down even farther in his seat. "I think I'm going crazy," he said flatly.

"And what does that mean?" she asked, glancing from the road to him.

He wanted her help desperately—for her to say that one special thing that moms were famous for—that one thing that puts everything magically into perspective and miraculously makes things better. But in this case, he doubted it was possible. "My hallucinations have been getting worse," he said at last. "Much worse."

"Okay," she responded. "When we get home, we'll call Dr. Powell and—"

"No, you don't understand," Tom interrupted. "It's so bad that I'm having a hard time telling what's real from what's not."

His mother nodded in understanding. "We can deal with that," she tried to reassure him. "There's nothing we can't handle. You're going to be fine—trust me." She reached over and patted his leg. "Really, you're going to be all right."

"No." Tom shook his head. "No, I don't think so."

"Tom, that's no way to talk. We'll—"

"Where do you think I've been all night?" he blurted.

"I don't really know," she replied calmly. "I'm thinking that maybe you were having one of your attacks and you wandered out of the house—"

"I woke up in a motel in West Virginia, Mom, where I learned that I had been sent to kill a guy named Tremain because I'm some kind of assassin with a split personality and—"

"Tom, you really are scaring me." His mother pulled the car over to the side of the road and stopped. He could see that her hands were shaking as they moved over the curved plastic of the dark green steering wheel.

"*You're* scared?" he asked, his voice shaking, threatening to shatter like glass. He was on the verge of tears again, and that would be the final straw, to *cry* in front of his mother. "How do you think I feel? I was in some guy's motel room, Ma—I had a gun."

His mother leaned back against the headrest, breathing in and out deeply. It was one of the relaxation exercises he'd seen her do in the past when things were getting a little too intense. "Oh my God," she whispered once and then again.

He had no idea why, but he suddenly started to laugh. Maybe it was a nervous reaction, or maybe he was just slipping that much further down the slope to insanity, but suddenly Tom found his situation hilarious.

"I haven't even told you the best part." He was laughing even harder now, hot tears streaming from his eyes and running down his face. "I've got this other personality, and I think I can feel him inside me—and he's trying to get out." His laughter had turned to a high-pitched giggle as he rocked from side to side, caught up in his escalating hysteria. "Isn't that a riot?"

And then, as quickly as it had come upon him, it was over. He wiped at his still-leaking eyes, breathing deeply, and then glanced at his mother to find her staring back at him. Tears filled her eyes as well, and he became very aware of what he was putting her through.

"I'm so sorry." He lowered his head, ashamed, not wanting to see the unhappiness and disappointment in her eyes. "I wanted so badly to be normal—to be like all the other kids. I tried, I really did, but . . ."

She leaned over, and he felt her hand cup the back of his head, her fingers running lovingly through his hair. And he was reminded of the times after he'd been diagnosed with Quentin's when she would hold him in her lap, stroke his head, and assure him that everything was going to be just fine.

"I'm going to need you to be strong, Tom," she said as she gently caressed his head. "We're all going to have to be strong."

He looked up at her then and saw that she was no longer crying. There was a different look on her face now, a kind of light in her eyes that told him she had found her focus, her strength, and was ready to do whatever it took to help him.

"As long as we remain strong, we'll get through this."

And, looking deeply into her eyes, Tom believed her.

"I love you, Mom," he said, his voice cracking with emotion.

"I love you too," she answered, pulling him close to kiss the top of his head.

And it would have been one of the most comforting moments of his life if it weren't for the nagging sense of danger that he couldn't shake.

Madison had returned to her room and, although she hadn't wanted to, found herself sleeping fitfully until she heard the sound of a car engine next door.

Mr. Personality going off to work, she thought sarcastically, rolling off the bed and going to the window. She watched the green Corolla back down the driveway and out into the street. *What kind of job does he have anyway,* she wondered, *that would make him to go to the office so early on a Sunday morning?* She couldn't remember if Tom had ever mentioned it.

Reluctantly she returned to her bed. Something just wasn't right. She thought again about the look on Mr. Lovett's face when she'd mentioned seeing Tom leave in a van. It hadn't been just annoyance—a look she knew well. No, it had been something else.

He was definitely lying.

She turned over and buried her face deep in her pillow, trying not to be paranoid, but she knew what she had seen. Why would Mr. Lovett lie? Why wouldn't he want her to know that Tom had left the house?

For a while she lay there, drifting in that weird, timeless place between being awake and asleep, only to be roused again by the sound of a car next door. Shaking off the numbing haze, she returned to her perch at the window.

The Corolla was back, and Madison gasped as she watched Mrs. Lovett open the passenger door and help her son from the car. She wrapped an arm around his shoulders and led him toward the house. Tom was wearing all black, just like last night, but he was walking with a zombie-like stiffness.

Madison wanted to open the window, to yell down to them, ask if Tom was all right, but the sight of him looking so helpless froze her in place.

Mrs. Lovett kissed her son on the side of his head, pulling him closer as they carefully climbed the steps to the front door.

Madison stepped back from the window as the two disappeared into the house.

"What the hell is going on?" she asked herself, hurrying to put her shoes back on.

She was damned well going to find out.

Stepping through the doorway of his house was like crossing the finish line of the Boston Marathon. Tom could finally begin to shut down, but something kept him wired.

His father came out from the kitchen, cell phone clutched to his face. "He's here now," Tom heard him say. And as he wrapped up his conversation, Tom, for a moment, wondered who his father was talking to but became too distracted to ask the question.

"Tom," his dad said, clipping the tiny phone to his belt as he moved to join them in the living room. "You look like hell."

"He's okay," his mother replied as she helped him onto the couch. "Just a little out of sorts."

Tom leaned his head against the soft back of the couch, willing himself to relax. He was home now: *home*, where he could figure it all out—separate fact from fiction.

"Let me get you a glass of juice and your pills," his mother offered, going toward the kitchen.

"Where'd you go, Tom?" his father asked, standing in front of him. His mother had stopped in the doorway and silently watched them both. "Do you remember why you left the house?"

Tom shook his head. "I don't remember leaving the house." He dropped his hands limply to his sides. "Although I did spend some time in a log cabin in my head talking with an old man—Dr. Bernard Quentin, actually, about how I'm some kind of secret government weapon."

His father stared at him, emotionless.

"Oh, and I killed this doctor—in my assassin identity, of course—a few days ago. Apparently."

His mother moved to his father's side. "Maybe we should let him lie down for a while. . . ."

"Assassin?" his father asked incredulously, ignoring Tom's mother.

Tom nodded vigorously. "Yeah, and when I woke up this time, I was in some guy's motel room in West

Virginia. I was supposed to kill him too, I guess, but Dr. Quentin did something, so—"

"Stop it, Tom," his father snapped. "Can't you hear yourself—how crazy you sound?"

"Don't you think I know that?" Tom cried, his voice shaking. "But it's what I remember." He shifted on the couch and felt a sharp sting in his side. He pulled up his shirt, turning slightly to show off twin welts where the Taser had left its mark. "How do you think I got these?" he asked.

His father leaned down for a closer look. "Those are bug bites, Tom," he said matter-of-factly. "From what your mother says, you've been running around in the woods near the air force base. God knows what could have bit you out there."

Tom stood, bringing his wounds closer for his parents to examine, desperate for them to believe him. "No, they're burns from a Taser. They used it to knock me out. Really, look at them."

His father took him firmly by the shoulders and looked squarely in his eyes. "No, Tom. They're not Taser burns. You had a daymare, a real doozy from the sound of it. All these crazy things you're telling us are a product of your condition, no matter how real they might seem to you. Do you understand, Tom? None of it was real."

Tom remembered how his father always comforted him after a particularly bad daymare, sitting with him, telling him to think of the bizarre hallucinations as a kind of television show, one that that he was special enough to be part of. They had never seemed quite so bad after that . . . well, until now.

It's bullshit, said that same creepy voice he had heard inside his head at the airport, a voice that he now knew belonged to Tyler Garrett. The sudden words were like a crack of thunder in the middle of a peaceful night. Tom flinched.

"Hey, you all right?" his father asked, noticing his reaction, but Tom didn't answer. That overwhelming sense of foreboding was back.

His father gave him a quick, hard shake. "What's happening, son?"

Tom tried to smile as he focused on his father's concerned features. "Did I mention that I've started hearing voices?" he asked wryly, making a lame attempt at humor. The urge to run from the house made the muscles in his legs twitch. There was danger here, his new senses told him. But that was insane. *This* was where he was safe.

His dad glanced briefly at his mother, where she stood in the center of the living room, arms folded tightly across her chest, as though she were incredibly cold. Then he reached out to push Tom back down onto the couch. Tom reacted, his entire body tensing. And his father stepped back, an expression that could very well have been fear appearing on his face. Tom felt sick to his stomach.

"I'm sorry," he said, looking from his dad to his mom. "I . . . It isn't you. . . . I'm feeling things . . . crazy things. I think I might need to lie down." He moved around his father. "Maybe you should call Dr. Powell now."

Tom winced, his stomach twisting in knots as he continued to fight the urge to get away. This was insane. These were his parents, for God's sake, his house. What could possibly harm him here?

Get out now! the presence that was Tyler Garrett shrieked from his hiding place somewhere in Tom's brain.

"I think I'm going to throw up," Tom mumbled, pushing past his parents, heading toward the stairs.

They didn't move, appearing helpless, stunned by his behavior. If they only knew what he was going through, how his diseased brain was making him feel. It was all too much to deal with at the moment.

He had reached the staircase when he caught the muffled sound of a car door slamming outside.

Too late, Garrett's voice whispered, and Tom squinted his eyes shut, forcing it away.

"What was that?" he asked from the stairs, glancing to his parents. They looked at each other, a silent message seeming to pass between them.

"Was it a car?" The sense of alarm he'd been experiencing intensified, and it took all he had not to turn and run for the back door.

To escape.

Escape what? Tom wondered as he left the stairs, walking toward the front door.

"Tom?" his mother called out.

"Where are you going, Tom?" his father joined in.

"I have to see who's here," he said dreamily as he pulled open the door. The first thing he saw was the van parked across the end of the driveway.

A black van.

And two men—Crenshaw and Burt, slowly coming up the drive.

"Oh my God," he whispered, hardly able to believe his eyes.

Madison pulled the front door closed behind her, getting ready for another embarrassing exchange with her friend's parents. Even though it was none of her business, something wasn't right, and she had to find out what was going on or go out of her *freakin'* mind.

She stepped from the brick pathway to the grass, about to cross the lawn to the house next door, and stopped short. A black van was parked at the end of the Lovetts' driveway—the same van she had seen from her window the night before.

She saw two men heading up the driveway and was tempted to call out to them. Maybe she could get her answers from them and save herself another encounter with Tom's father. They hadn't seemed to notice her, so she resumed her trek across the lawn, watching them with great curiosity as she went.

As they neared the Lovetts' front door, each reached inside his loose-fitting black jacket and removed something. At first she thought her eyes were playing tricks on her, because, seriously, why would two men be at Tom's house with guns? It was absolutely crazy.

But absolutely true.

Madison froze. Her first instinct was to use her cell phone to call 911, but as her hand moved to where her pocket should have been, she remembered she was still wearing her sweats, and her cell was on the dresser back in her room.

She was about to turn and run back to her aunt and uncle's house to call the police from there when she saw the Lovetts' front door open.

"Tom," she said in a frightened whisper, seeing him standing in the entryway.

And before she really knew what she was doing, Madison was running across the lawn toward him.

CHAPTER 13

Tom looked from the two men slowly advancing up the drive to his parents standing perfectly still in the living room.

"They're coming," he said in a voice tainted by terror, quickly closing the door. "You've got to do something—call the police. They're outside."

His mother and father didn't move. They simply stared at him as though he had lost his mind.

"Look, this is real!" he shouted, pointing at the door. "The men who tried to take me . . ." He pulled up his shirt to expose the Taser welts again. "The men who did this, they're coming!"

"Tom, let us help you," his father said calmly, moving toward him.

They still didn't believe him. Their very lives were in danger and here they were, standing around, sad that their only child had lost his mind.

"Look! Tom screamed, pulling open the door again. "Look for yourselves—I'm not crazy."

The two men were closer now, guns drawn.

"We've got to do something!" He reached for his father's cell phone, but his dad's hand blocked his own.

"It's okay, Tom," his father said. "Everything is going to be fine."

"But they're coming." Tom's voice was growing higher with panic. "They have guns and . . ."

And then his father did the unthinkable—he raised a hand in greeting.

"What are you doing?" Tom asked incredulously, looking from his father back to the armed men in the driveway.

Burt and Crenshaw waved back, as if they were all old friends.

Tom couldn't believe his eyes. "Dad, what are you doing?" he asked again.

His father remained silent.

"Mom, you have to do something," Tom begged, trying to push past his father into the living room.

His father's hand fell firmly on his shoulder, stopping him. "Tom," he said. "Mom and I are going to help you."

His mother stepped into the foyer. "Listen to your

father," she said with a strained smile. "This is for your own good."

It was as if he'd been stabbed by the world's biggest knife, the blade stuck deep within his gut, all his blood—his life—draining away and leaving him empty.

His parents—they were part of the madness too.

It would be so much easier to put his fate in the hands of someone else, to stop fighting, to give in, he thought.

So easy.

Tom tried to ignore the instincts that shrieked at him to run away and turned his attention to Burt and Crenshaw. He could see that Crenshaw's nose was swollen, his nostrils stained with blood from where Tom had hit him in their struggle at the airfield.

"They're going to kill me," Tom warned, knowing in his gut that what he was saying was absolutely true. And then he caught sight of Madison running headlong across the lawn.

You know they'll kill her too, don't you? the voice of his double asked.

"Tom!" she called out, and at the sound of her voice the two men in the driveway began to turn, weapons aimed.

What're you gonna do, boy? Garrett prodded. But Tom knew the answer before the question was even asked. He could never allow them to hurt her because of him.

It was a strange sensation then, as if his brain were expanding, filling up with things—as if a dam had been blown open, allowing a deluge of information to flood his consciousness, threatening to drown him.

He left the doorway just as the two men turned toward Madison. They were beside his mother's car as he reached them. Crenshaw must have heard him coming, pivoting his body, nine-millimeter Beretta ready to fire. Tom saw the man's movement as if in slow motion, considering a number of options as the weapon continued to its optimal firing position.

He was shocked by the things he seemed to know. There were at least thirteen ways he could remove the gun from Crenshaw's hand; three even allowed the man to keep his life. Tom chose what he thought would be the quickest and least damaging, and suddenly he seemed to be moving at superspeed. He stepped forward, took hold of Crenshaw's wrist, and, twisting the gun away, drove his elbow into the side of the gunman's face. He plucked the gun from Crenshaw's hand as he fell to the driveway unconscious and aimed it at Burt.

Not bad, an approving voice praised from somewhere inside his head.

Madison was standing perfectly still as Burt trained his own weapon on her. "Drop the gun or I'll shoot her," he croaked, and Tom could see that a fine sheen of sweat dappled the man's brow and upper lip. He was afraid, and could you blame him? From what Tom knew about Tyler Garrett, he was certainly a person to be frightened of.

Tom started to smile, squinting down the barrel of the Beretta. "Go ahead, and then I'll shoot you," he said, startled by the cruelty of his statement.

His eyes locked with Madison's and he felt his heart lurch. She was terrified, even more in the dark than he was. Then he heard the scuffle of feet on blacktop, and he turned to see his parents leaving the house.

"Tom, what are you doing?" his mother screeched.

It was the opportunity that Burt had been waiting for: as Tom turned back to the gunman, he saw that the van driver had changed his target from Madison to him.

Tom felt the hint of tension build in his trigger finger but resisted the urge to shoot. Instead he flipped the gun in his hand and threw it with incredible precision, hitting Burt squarely between the eyes. The man fell backward with a grunt, his gun firing once into the air as he fell to the ground.

Seeing that the man was down and out, Tom sprinted down the driveway to Madison.

"What the hell is happening?" she demanded as he grabbed her by the wrist, yanking her toward the driver's side of his mother's car.

"We have to get out of here," he stated firmly, pulling open the door and forcing her inside. She didn't fight, sliding across to the passenger side.

His parents yelled for him to stop, but he ignored them. They were somehow part of all this, and he couldn't bear to listen to any more of their lies—to even look at them. He had to get out of here, pull his thoughts together.

"Please, tell me what's going on," Madison pleaded. "Are you in some kind of trouble? Who are those people? If you don't start talking to me right away, I think I'm going to scream."

He looked over at her, keeping his expression and tone as calm as possible. "As soon as we're away from here, I'll tell you everything I know, I swear." He truly hated the fact that she had become involved, but there was nothing he could do about it now except try and keep her safe.

His father pounded on the hood of the car, causing him to jump, while his mother had approached the driver's side and was rapping on the window glass, trying to get him to look at her. "Please, Tom, come out of there," she begged.

He refused to look at her, turning his attention to the steering column.

"What are we going to do now?" Madison asked, her voice trembling.

"We get out of here fast," Tom replied tightly.

"Do you have the keys?"

"Won't need them." With the flat of his hand he struck the plastic cylinder encircling the steering column, cracking it open to expose the multicolored wires beneath. Leaning to the left and gazing under the steering wheel, he found the two ignition wires. It was if he had somehow stepped back and was watching someone else detach and strip the two wires, tying them together. The engine rumbled to life.

Tom put the car in reverse, glancing momentarily at Madison, who was staring at him, mouth open.

"Where did you learn to do that?"

"Later," he said as he stepped on the gas. "Besides, you wouldn't believe me anyway."

His mother and father leapt out of the way as the car shot down the slight incline.

"The van's blocking our way," Madison offered, quickly putting her seat belt on.

"Temporarily," Tom answered coolly, feeling that same kind of emotional detachment he had felt while hot wiring the car.

Crenshaw was up now, blood dripping down his face from his re-injured nose. He had managed to retrieve Burt's gun and stood at the side of the driveway, aiming at the Toyota. Tom turned the wheel slightly, forcing the man to dive out of the way. Then the back end of the Toyota struck the van at the end of the driveway with a crash, pushing it out into the street.

"Hold on," he told Madison, putting the car in drive and pulling forward. His parents stood in the driveway, as if daring him to strike them. Tom suddenly saw the life he'd had with them flash before his eyes, feeling like he'd just found out he was an unknowing participant in some kind of bizarre reality television show and this was the series finale.

It was all a lie.

His anger flared as if doused with gasoline, and he struggled with the idea of running them both down, but as much as part of him would have liked to, he simply did not have the time.

Tom hit the brakes, slammed the car in reverse again, and sent it barreling down the driveway into the van for a final time. His back end was practically nonexistent now, but he was able to maneuver around the obstruction. Throwing the car into drive and with tires screeching, he carried out their escape.

Tom reached the end of the cul-de-sac, banging a

sharp right onto the main road. He could feel Madison staring at him. She was pressed up against the passenger door.

"We're going someplace where we can talk," he said quietly. "And I promise I can prove to you that I'm not crazy."

Time stood still for Victoria in the driveway of her home. Calmly she took it all in, reviewing the events that had just occurred with crystal clarity.

It happened so fast.

There was a man on all fours just ahead, like a dog, blood streaming from a nasty gash on his forehead. Another man paced at the driveway's end, talking on a cell phone, his voice raised excitedly. Victoria found his movement strangely mesmerizing: back and forth, back and forth.

She looked past the pacing man to the van now sideways across the width of the street in front of her house. *That will need to be moved,* she thought, making a mental note of the things that should be taken care of immediately.

She felt like one of the victims of a natural disaster that she'd seen so many times on the nightly news, women and men standing amid the wreckage of their homes, their eyes strangely vacant.

From this moment on, things will never be the same.

Out of the corner of her eye she saw that Mason had come to stand beside her. He was wearing that look as well, a glazed expression of shock. She had grown quite fond of her partner over time and reached out to take his hand.

"We'll get through this," she said quietly, giving his hand a gentle squeeze, hoping to infuse him with some of her strength.

He turned his attention away from the aftermath of their very own natural disaster to look at her. And for a moment she felt that he believed her, that they could handle the problem on their own. But then the look of hope drained away, replaced by one of trepidation as Mason released her hand and removed the cell phone from his belt.

"We have to make the call," he said, his thumb already beginning to punch in the numbers.

Victoria wasn't the least bit religious; how could she be, really, after all she had seen in her life, but for a moment she prayed for some kind of intervention, anything to buy them time to pool their thoughts and decide their next, best course of action. But her request to a higher power was denied, and she knew it would be pointless to ask her partner to delay the call. He had always been a stickler for protocol.

"Good morning, Mr. Kavanagh," Mason Lovett said into the phone. "This is Handler One. We have a situation."

An unfinished home in the Orchard Place housing development proved to be exactly what they were looking for.

They had entered the abandoned construction site from an incomplete back entrance, on a rutted road of sand and dirt, hiding the Toyota inside the shell of a two-car garage and seeking shelter in the half-finished building to which it was attached.

Tom vaguely remembered hearing his parents talk about this development. The same guy had built the homes on Tom's own cul-de-sac, but here the developer had bypassed certain environmental laws. He had already started building the multimillion-dollar homes when the state shut him down for infringing on the rights of an endangered species of bird that nested somewhere nearby. He had tried to fight the decision but had eventually gone bankrupt, leaving behind a partially developed site that would never see completion.

Inside one of these homes, in what would likely have been the master bedroom, Tom leaned back against the plasterboard wall and watched as Madison retreated to the far corner of the room.

"Nice place you've got here," she said warily, stepping over a pile of trash probably left behind by some partyers. She was trying to make light of the situation, but the tremble in her voice gave it all away. She was scared.

"Yeah," he responded, looking around the room. "A little paint on the walls and it'll be good to go."

She smiled briefly, then looked away. "So what now?" she asked, folding her arms tightly across her chest.

Tom slid down the wall to the unfinished floor, removed his glasses, and rubbed at his aching eyes. "I guess I need to tell you what's going on . . . or at least what I think is going on, but I'm realizing how crazy it all sounds."

Madison sat down as well but maintained a safe distance across from him. "Why don't you let me be the judge of crazy?" she suggested. "What I've been through so far this morning has been pretty nuts, so I'm open to just about anything at this point."

Tom leaned his head back against the wall, feeling the coolness of the plaster on his scalp. He was about to put his glasses back on but suddenly realized that he could see better without them. He folded them up and slipped them into his jacket pocket.

"Okay, here goes," Tom said, taking a deep breath.

"You remember the other night, I was telling you about the bizarre dreams that people who have narcolepsy sometimes get?"

Madison nodded. "You called them hypnagogic hallucinations, right?"

If things weren't so awful at the moment, he would have been psyched—she'd actually been listening to him. "That's right," he continued. "Well, a few nights ago I had this dream—this hallucination of an old man being murdered in a cabin." He paused, not really wanting to go on but knowing he had no choice. "I killed the man." He watched the expression on Madison's face for signs of change. "But it wasn't really me," he added quickly.

He ran a hand through his hair and exhaled loudly. "This is where it gets a little confusing."

Madison remained silent, waiting. Listening.

"I had another hallucination where I actually spoke to the old man, and he told me that it wasn't a dream at all, that he was a . . . an implant, a kind of program put inside my head in case something happened to him. He said his name was Dr. Quentin—"

"Quentin?" Madison interrupted.

Tom nodded. "Bernard Quentin. The guy who first discovered Quentin's narcolepsy; he was the old man in my dreams. Why?"

"Last night," she explained. "I saw it on the news. He's missing. He'd been at his cabin in Maine, but no one's heard from him. Now you're saying that you—"

"I'm connected," Tom finished. What he had hoped was madness was gradually being exposed as reality. He felt like he was falling and wondered when he would hit the ground.

Madison stood up, eyeing him cautiously. "So you're telling me that you killed this doctor . . . then talked to him after he was murdered?"

"Wait," Tom begged. "I know it sounds like bullshit; I told you it would. I guess Quentin was involved in some kind of government project to create . . ." He hesitated.

Assassins, offered his other half.

"Assassins," Tom finished. "He thought he was doing work to help cure Quentin's narcolepsy, but in fact they were incorporating his research into a program where children with the disease had other personalities put inside their heads." Tom slowly rubbed his temple with one of his hands.

"They wanted two separate personalities living inside one mind—the ultimate sleeper agent, a killer who wasn't even aware that he was one. I guess those of us with Quentin's narcolepsy are more susceptible or something."

Madison was slowly sliding along the wall, trying to act casual as she moved toward the doorway. "So you're some kind of government agent?"

He caught the disbelief in her voice and really couldn't blame her.

"No, *I'm* not," he said, unable to keep the exasperation out of his own voice, desperate for her to understand. "It's the other half of me—the one in my head. *He's* the agent—the killer. Not me."

Tom got to his feet as she darted toward the exit. "Please, Madison," he begged. "Let me finish. Let me prove it." She watched him from the doorway as he walked to the corner farthest from her and squatted. "Please," he asked again, gesturing for her to come back into the room, and eventually she did, watching him with a cautious eye.

"I'll stay right here," she said, leaning against the wall by the door. "Unless the guy inside your head doesn't approve."

Tom tried again to make her understand, though he wasn't quite sure that even he knew what was happening to him. "The message left by Quentin did something to the barriers inside my head. I know about my other personality now, and he knows about me."

Madison laughed nervously. "Do you hear yourself?

215

Do you actually expect me to buy what you're trying to sell here?"

Tom said nothing, not wanting to sound crazier than he already did.

"The sad thing is that I think you actually believe this story," Madison continued. "That all this stuff about government experiments and assassins is actually true, but tell me this, Tom Lovett, how do you know it's not another one of your hallucinations? You yourself said it was hard to tell them from reality; how can you be sure it isn't just some crazy dream?"

Tom reached down and snatched up a bottle cap, bouncing it in his hand. "I know," he said simply.

"Prove it," she replied.

Tom pointed to his face. "I don't need my glasses anymore—because *he* doesn't need glasses to see."

She didn't look convinced.

"And the car—I hot-wired a car, Madison."

"Yeah, and how do I know you just didn't learn that on the Inter—"

"I don't know how to drive," Tom interrupted. "My parents wouldn't teach me because of my condition, but somehow I did just fine."

Madison folded her arms, her brow furrowing in concentration.

"What about those guys at my house?" Tom asked

her. "Those were definitely real guns they were going to use to shoot you."

The look on her face was almost comical, as if for a moment she had actually forgotten about them. "So, who were they?" she asked.

"They were transport, in charge of getting me to and from my missions. I wasn't even supposed to know that I'd left my house, but whatever Quentin did, it woke me up while I was on a mission to kill some government guy."

"And did you?" she asked suspiciously.

Tom shook his head. "No. The guy . . ."

Tremain. The name popped into his head. *Christian Tremain.*

"His name was Tremain, and he seemed to know what I was. He said he wanted to help me."

"So why didn't he?" she challenged.

"I panicked," Tom said quietly. "I didn't know what was happening, and I ran. Got picked up by Burt and Crenshaw and flown back to Butler."

"Burt and Crenshaw?"

"The guys in the driveway."

Madison nodded as if everything now made perfect sense. If only that were the case. "And why, again, were they after you?"

"When they picked me up, I was me, not Garrett."

217

"Garrett?"

"The assassin. Tyler Garrett is his name."

"Your other personality," she added.

Tom nodded.

Madison turned to the side and kicked at some trash on the floor. She shook her head in disbelief and turned back to face him. "Everything you've told me is absolutely crazy," she began slowly. "There shouldn't be any doubt in my mind that you're a nut job."

Tom nodded. "Believe me, I know. If only there was some way . . ."

He paused, yet another piece of information rising slowly to the surface of his thoughts. It was almost as if Garrett was trying to help him.

"Tom?" Madison called. "What's wrong?"

"There's a way I can prove what I'm saying is true."

"Okay," she said carefully. "How's that?"

"There . . . there's a transmitter in my body," he said slowly. "It's used to track my whereabouts, just in case I should go missing. They spent a lot of money on me and don't want to lose their investment," he explained. He got up and began to look through the trash on the floor, talking as he searched. "Remove the transmitter and you'll have proof." He reached down and picked up a bent nail and offered it to Madison. "Here, you can use this."

Madison looked confused. "For what?"

Tom shrugged out of his coat and got down on his knees, pulling up his T-shirt to expose his back. "You're going to have to break the skin to get at the tracking device," he explained.

"You—you want me to cut you with this?" she stammered.

"It's the only way," Tom replied. "There should be a scar near my right shoulder blade. I remember getting it when I was eight years old. I fell on a piece of glass. I was using a chair to get a box of cookies off the top shelf above the sink and I lost my balance. I knocked a glass off the counter as I fell, and . . ." He paused.

"What?" Madison asked, behind him.

"I guess that never really happened," he whispered sadly. He turned his head to look at her. "I wonder how much more of what I remember never really happened."

And then he felt her hand on the bare skin of his back, the warmth of her tremulous breath tickling his neck, and suddenly he was no longer concerned with the past but only with the reality of the moment.

"Are . . . are you cold?" she asked in a tentative whisper. "You're shaking."

"I'm fine," he stated, attempting to keep his emotions

in check. He was surprised at his body's reaction to her. Even after all he'd been through—was going through.

"What should I do?" she asked.

He tingled all over, sensing the closeness of her presence.

"Use the point of the nail to break the skin," he directed.

"But . . . the nail is rusty and . . ."

"Don't worry about it," he assured her. "It'll be fine. I'll risk having to get a tetanus shot if it's going to prove that I'm not out of my mind."

He felt the cold point of the nail press down on his flesh and instinctively tensed the muscles in his back.

"I don't know if I can do this," Madison stated, lifting the nail from his skin.

"You can do it, Madison. You *have* to do it, for both our sakes."

He felt the tip of the nail again and winced at its sharp bite as she pressed it down into his skin. "If it helps, think of this as a really weird first date," he said through gritted teeth.

She didn't respond to his attempt at humor, continuing to dig into the layers of scar tissue.

"You're bleeding," she said finally.

"Grab that napkin over there," he told her.

And she did so, snatching up the crumpled paper

from the trash on the floor and dabbing at the wound. "I don't see anything," she said.

"Keep digging. They probably put it in deep so it wouldn't be noticed."

"Tom, there's nothing here," Madison said, and he could hear the exasperation creeping into her tone.

"It's there," he stated assertively, the burning pain in his shoulder blade radiating outward across his back.

"It's not," she cried, her voice beginning to quaver.

"You need to go deeper," Tom said, regretting the words as they left his mouth.

"I can't." She was clearly on the verge of tears.

"Do what I tell you, damn it!" Tom screamed, a surge of anger bubbling up from some hidden reserve.

Madison shoved the nail into him, and he nearly screamed again when it broke through the next layer of tender tissue. Explosions of color bloomed before his eyes, and he felt himself becoming light-headed.

"Oh my God," he heard Madison suddenly say.

"What is it?" he asked, craning his neck to see.

"I think I see something." She continued to dig, dabbing at the wound with the blood-soaked napkin.

"Hurry." He breathed in and out deeply, trying to block out the pain. "I'm not sure how much longer . . ."

Tom pitched forward to the ground, his face pressed to the filthy wooden floor.

"I've got it," Madison said excitedly, probing deeper and deeper into the meat of his shoulder, using her fingers to explore the gash.

Tom couldn't help himself. "No more," he cried out, rolling away from her. His back was wet with blood and sweat.

Madison was on her knees, holding something about the size of one of his pills in her bloodstained fingertips. "I've got it," she said almost dreamily. "It was there, just like you said. . . ." Her voice trailed off as the weight of realization came crashing down on her.

Tom reached out and grabbed the transmitter, slick with blood. He placed it on the ground, then got to his feet and quickly stomped on it with the heel of his sneaker.

But he realized that his action was a little too late as he heard the sounds of multiple footfalls rumbling through the house.

"Tom?" Madison questioned, jumping to her feet to stand at his side.

He looked toward the window opening as a way for them to escape, but a man in black, his face hidden by a ski mask, had beaten them to it. Madison screamed as he leveled his assault weapon at them. Tom saw that it was a Special Operations Combat Assault Rifle, SCAR for short. Whoever had called in this assault wasn't taking any chances. Two more masked soldiers moved into the room, their assault weapons at the ready as well.

"Keep your hands where I can see them," one of the men bellowed, and Madison jumped closer to Tom, grabbing hold of his hand.

Faced with this latest threat, the presence inside was again stirred, surging to the front of his brain, clawing to be free. How easy it would be to lose control of it, Tom thought. Multiple scenarios of intense violence exploded in his mind, showing him what was likely to happen and how he should react.

The armed men moved cautiously closer, and Tom could tell they knew he—Garrett—could be a threat to them.

"Get down on the floor with your hands behind your head," one of the gunmen yelled, staring intensely down the barrel of his weapon.

The lead soldier suddenly rushed forward, driving the butt of his rifle into Tom's solar plexus, dropping him to his knees.

Madison screamed in protest as the other gunman roughly tore her away from him.

Hunched over, clutching at his aching stomach,

Tom knew that they were out of options. If he and Madison were to survive, he had to give in to the strange and alien force that he could feel struggling deep inside him. He had to let it out.

No matter how much it scared him to do so.

Madison's mind was racing.

I've got to be on something, she thought feverishly. *Someone's slipped me something without me knowing and I'm, like, tripping or something.*

It was the only explanation that made any kind of sense.

Her arm was being held by a masked soldier toting a machine gun. Tom was on his knees in front of the other soldier, coughing and gagging because he'd just been hit in the stomach with the butt of an assault rifle.

Yep, drugs. Has to be, or maybe it's a fever dream.

Madison closed her eyes and counted to five, wishing with all her might that she'd wake up on the floor of somebody's house, trying to recover from a wild night of partying. But deep down she knew it wouldn't happen. Somehow this was real: the smell of the soldier's nervous sweat, the stickiness of Tom's drying blood on her hands, and the tortured sounds of his pain-racked coughs told her that it was all true.

All real.

The masked soldier who had aimed at them through the window outside had joined the party, entering the room with a confident swagger. "We got them," he said. There was an excitement in his voice.

The soldier standing over Tom nodded, his gaze never leaving the helpless boy. "We sure did."

But the words had no sooner left his mouth than Tom suddenly sprang up from his knees, moving so fast that Madison's eyes could barely keep up.

"You don't have shit," she heard him growl as he took hold of the soldier's machine gun, grabbing it by the barrel and angling the eruption of gunfire away from himself. And then the soldier was suddenly coughing and choking, clutching at his throat. He fell to the ground, but Tom was already on the move, hurling himself across the room toward another of their attackers.

If she had thought the situation was scary before, now she was utterly terrified.

Madison's captor threw her roughly against the back wall, running to help his team. She fell to the ground, the wind knocked from her lungs, watching the fight unfolding in stunned silence.

It was hard to accept Tom's crazy story about split personalities and assassins inside his head, even after finding the transmitter hidden beneath the skin of his shoulder. *It was all so crazy.*

But seeing him now, the way he stood, swaying on the balls of his feet, the slightest hint of a smile on his face, he *did* seem like a different person than the one she'd had ice cream with the previous night.

Madison had no choice but to believe.

All so crazy real.

It was a surreal feeling, suddenly knowing how to do things that he would never have imagined himself capable of. Tom was amazed and even a little excited as he prepared to deal with the soldiers sent to apprehend him. He could hear Tyler Garrett's thoughts, cold and efficient and frighteningly matter-of-fact, as he explained how to take out the soldiers, one after another.

Take the leader first and watch the morale of the others crumble. Tom sprang into action. He grabbed hold of the muzzle of the machine gun held by the soldier who had hit him in the stomach and simply pushed it aside. Then he drove his outstretched fingers into the soldier's throat, nearly collapsing his windpipe. He was moving on to his next opponent before the choking soldier even hit the floor.

The last soldier to enter had raised his weapon and was preparing to fire, but Tom was already spinning a leg around to swat the machine gun from the man's hands with his foot. The soldier pulled a knife from a sheath strapped to his boot, driving Tom back—into the waiting arms of the gunman who had been guarding Madison.

Tom felt himself crushed in a powerful bear hug, but his mind remained surprisingly calm, calculating his follow-through as if he was doing a math problem. He shifted his body to one side, throwing the man behind him off balance. Then he tossed his head backward, driving the back of his skull into the man's chin with enough force to stun him into loosening his grip.

The one with the knife came at him full tilt, but Tom wasn't the least bit concerned. He had briefly turned around, relieving the man behind him of his sidearm. With cold-hearted efficiency he shot him once in the chest and with one fluid motion spun around to fire another round into the man with the knife.

The gunshots were like cracks of thunder within the confined space, their dull roar just beginning to fade as Madison started to scream.

"What are you doing?" she cried, staring at him with a disturbing mixture of disgust and horror. "You didn't have to kill them."

Tom lowered the gun, his feverish thought process beginning to slow now that the threat had been neutralized. "I know that, and I didn't."

He walked over to one of the felled men, pointing out a smoldering hole in the center of his chest. There was no blood.

"They're all wearing body armor," he explained. "The force of the bullet just knocked the wind out of their sails. They'll be pretty bruised but fine."

An overpowering urge to murder the soldiers came on him in a sudden flash. "But . . . but we can't allow them to recover."

Tom found himself taking aim at the nearest soldier on the floor. "If they do, they'll be a danger to us all over again."

It made perfect sense as his finger tightened on the trigger.

"Tom?"

The soft, fear-filled voice suddenly distracted him from the horror of what he was about to do. Tom looked toward Madison, using the same strength and determination he had developed over the years in struggling with his affliction to overpower his darker side, forcing it down—forcing it to the back of his consciousness and allowing himself to regain control.

Tom dropped to his knees before a frightened Madison.

"Tom," she asked again cautiously. "Is . . . is it you or . . ."

He opened his eyes and looked down at the hand that still held the pistol.

"It's me," he said, letting the weapon tumble to the floor. "Thank God it's me."

Marty Arsenault opened one bleary eye and listened. The air conditioner continued to hum noisily as it had since he'd put it in the window during that ridiculously hot spell in the middle of May, the prevalent sound in their often-stuffy bedroom. Marty loved the AC, loved the chill it put in the air, allowing him to wrap himself in a blanket cocoon all year round, and especially loved the buffer it *usually* provided from the sounds of the outdoors.

Goddamned birds, he thought, not sure if it was indeed his winged enemies that had woken him, but he had heard something.

Rolling over, he looked at his wife and found her still fast asleep. He pulled the covers around himself and was about to dive back into the arms of unconsciousness when he heard the noise again.

Somebody was ringing the doorbell.

He thought about ignoring it, then worried that it might be something important. He sat up and again gazed at his sleeping wife, wondering if he should wake her. After all, misery did love company. But he decided not to; maybe she'd return the favor someday. He'd be sure to tell her later all about how he'd let her stay asleep while he got up from a nice cozy bed to answer the door.

Marty got up, slipped his feet into his slippers, and grabbed his robe. Opening the bedroom door, he padded stiffly out into the hallway. He glanced toward the guest room, where Madison was staying. *It would take an atom bomb to wake her up,* he thought, heading for the stairs.

The chimes of the doorbell were ringing again, and he quickened his step. *This better be good,* a cranky voice inside his head squawked.

"All right, all right," he muttered under his breath as the bell rang yet another time.

Marty looked through the peephole but could see nothing. Then he remembered that Ellen had hung a summer wreath recently. Making sure that his bathrobe was tied tight, Marty unlocked the door and pulled it open.

At first he didn't recognize the man and woman standing on his doorstep. Assuming they were Jehovah's Witnesses, he was about to abruptly close the door when the man stepped forward.

"It's Marty, right?" he said, sticking out his hand.

A spark of recognition burned through the still-lingering fog of sleep, and Marty nodded at his neighbors. He'd seen them so rarely in person that he barely knew their faces. He opened the door wide and smiled apologetically.

"Victoria and Mason," the man continued with a good-natured laugh, pointing to his wife.

Marty nodded. "Yeah, from next door. Sorry, I'm still half asleep. What's up?"

Mason stepped closer, pulling a gun from the small of his back and pointing it at Marty's stomach.

"Wha—wha—?" Marty stammered, unable to take his eyes from the weapon.

"What's this all about?" Mason suggested casually. "Why don't you invite us in and we'll discuss it."

"Are they secure?" Tom asked Madison as he cinched the plastic restraints, which had likely been intended for them, around the wrists of one of the soldiers. He checked to be certain that the bonds were tight but not too tight and looked over to see how she was doing.

Madison knelt beside the two men who were lying on their stomachs, their hands bound behind their backs. "Yeah," she said. "I think so."

"Good." Tom hauled his charge up by the shoulders and leaned him back against the wall. The soldier was conscious now, eyes blazing with hate through the holes of the black ski mask he wore. This was the one Tom had taken down first, the one who had been the recipient of the finger thrust to the throat. His breathing was still a little wheezy.

Tom reached out and pulled the mask from his face, revealing a man in his mid- to late thirties, hair cut very short in a military style. He snarled at Tom like some kind of wild animal that had been caught in a trap.

"What are you going to do?" Madison asked, coming to stand beside him.

"I'm going to ask him some questions," Tom replied. "I want to know what they're up to—I need to know what's coming next."

The soldier said nothing, continuing to stare menacingly with his intensely dark eyes.

Tom already knew that the man was not going to talk willingly, that he had been trained to hold his tongue, and besides, it was a matter of principle. He wasn't going to talk to the guy who had kicked his ass.

"Maybe we should just leave them and go," Madison suggested.

Tom stood and walked to the center of the room. "I wish we could, but this guy knows things—things that can help us get out of this mess alive."

The killer inside him was stirring again, roused by the chance of violence. It knew what needed to be done to ensure his and Madison's safety, and it shared this information happily, a static whisper inside his mind.

Tom picked up the knife from the floor, where it had fallen earlier in the struggle.

Images of unthinkable things he had learned—*no, that Tyler Garrett had learned*—to do with a knife very much like this erupted in his brain.

"I . . . I know some ways to get this guy to talk," he said, the horrible knowledge making him feel a little sick.

Tom returned to kneel in front of the defiantly silent man, holding up the glinting steel blade for him to see.

"I want you to listen to me very closely," he told the man as he concentrated on the blade in his hand. "I have no desire to hurt you, but the other guy—the one who lives inside my head?" Tom looked from the knife into the soldier's eyes. "You know what he can do."

The soldier said nothing, but there was a change in his expression that let Tom know he realized exactly what he was facing.

"He's told me things," Tom said calmly. "Things that I could do with this knife."

Tom held his breath, hoping that the assassin's reputation would psych the soldier into telling him what he wanted to know.

But the man remained silently defiant.

"One involves your fingernails, how to slip the blade under the nails to slowly pry them off." Tom demonstrated, pretending to do the horrific deed to an imaginary hand. "And that's just a warm-up. I don't even want to tell you what he wants me to do with your eyelids."

The soldier swallowed hard, closing his eyes and exhaling loudly.

"I just want to know what's next," Tom said. He lowered the blade, waiting for an answer.

The soldier opened his eyes and a smirk slowly spread across his features. "Don't worry. You'll know soon enough."

The anger Tom felt was sudden and intense, and it reinforced his beliefs that Tyler Garrett's rage was somehow leaking into his.

"You son of a bitch," he spat, grabbing the man by

the shoulder and tipping him forward to the ground.

"Tom, what are you doing?" Madison asked, a hint of panic in her voice.

"I'm sorry, but it has to be done," he said as he brought the knife to the man's hands, still fastened behind his back. "I gave him every opportunity, but he wants to be a hard-ass. He's left me no choice."

Most of him was bluffing as he grabbed hold of the soldier's thumb and pressed the tip of the knife blade under the nail, but there was a part of Tom that really wasn't. A part of him that knew he might have to do something unspeakably horrible if he and Madison were going to survive this. He just hoped it wouldn't come to that.

But it might, Garrett whispered, *and that's when you and I become that much more alike.*

Tom leaned in close to the man's ear, making him very aware of where the blade was placed. "Tell me what I need to know or I turn you over to him."

The soldier's struggles lessened, the defiance seeming to leak from his body. "All right, all right," he said. "What does it matter anyway? You and the girl are already dead; you're just too stupid to realize it."

Tom flipped the man onto his back. "Yeah, we're really stupid, which is why I need some answers." He pressed the blade to the man's neck, taking a perverse pleasure in the fear that appeared on his face. "What's going to happen?"

"The operation here has been blown. It's only a matter of time before Pandora sends in its task force."

"Pandora?" Madison questioned. "Who's that?"

The soldier scoffed. "See? Real stupid."

Tom nicked the side of the man's face with the knife, and he yelped in pain as a bubble of crimson leaked from the wound.

"Whoops," Tom said. "Stupid mistake; hope I don't make another. Go on."

"Nothing much more to tell," the soldier grumbled. "Our job was to apprehend you if possible—to terminate you if necessary—before Pandora arrived. The handlers were to take care of sanitation at the base of operations."

The handlers. Tom's hand twitched, cutting the soldier's face again, accidentally this time.

"Why'd you do that?" he screeched, a new trickle of blood leaking from a much-deeper gash in his cheek. "I'm telling you everything I know."

"Sanitation," Tom spat. "For the benefit of us stupid people, what exactly does that mean?"

"It means sanitation," the man replied, obviously aggravated. "To sanitize—to eliminate any evidence that you existed, standard procedure for any operation gone sour."

"How would they do that?" he asked, knowing he wouldn't like the answer.

The man thought for a moment. "Usually by fire." He shrugged. "They make it look like an accident. The base of operation—in this case, your home—is burnt to the ground, as are any other homes in the area. It's not good business to leave any loose ends."

Madison gasped, and Tom looked up to see her backing toward the door.

"Madison, wait," he called out.

"My aunt and uncle," she said in a terrified whisper. Then she turned, running from the house.

"Madison!"

Tom ran out of the house just in time to see Madison climbing into the Toyota and slamming the door closed. He rushed over to the car, but she had already locked the doors.

"Madison, please. We need to talk. Don't do this. It's not safe."

Tom watched her through the glass as she bent down in the front seat, fiddling with the wires that dangled from the steering column.

Tom jumped back as the engine roared to life.

Madison looked at him through the driver's side

window. "I'm sorry," she yelled as she put the car in drive. "But you're part of this—and watching you with those soldiers . . . I'm not sure I can trust you."

The back tires spun out in the dirt, a cloud of exhaust and dust choking the air. Tom stood there stunned as the car finally gripped the unfinished road and sped off.

Madison wasn't really sure what to expect.

She had parked the car on Stanley Place, a street that ran parallel to the cul-de-sac where her aunt and uncle lived, and then cut through some backyards on foot to end up behind their home.

Squatting down in some tall grass and shrubs, she watched the back of the house for a few minutes and saw nothing out of the ordinary. She had fully expected to see both her aunt and uncle's house, as well as Tom's, in flames or something equally as horrible, but both seemed perfectly fine.

Cautiously she emerged from her hiding place and crossed the backyard to the deck. As quietly as she could, Madison crept up to the sliding glass door. Peering into the kitchen, she saw that it was empty and tested the door with a tug. It slid open on its track, and

Madison silently thanked her uncle for not paying attention to her aunt's constant nagging to keep it locked.

She stepped into the kitchen and was nearly overwhelmed by the smell of gas. Her hand immediately went to her mouth and nose, and it took everything she had not to start coughing from the smell of rotting eggs. She could hear a hissing sound from the stove and quickly went to it. All the burner controls were turned to the off position, and she couldn't quite figure where the sound of escaping gas was coming from. Then she noticed that the stove had been moved; it had been pushed away from the wall slightly. Hopping up on the counter, careful not to bang her head on the overhanging cabinet, she craned her neck to look behind the stove. The gas line had been disconnected.

Sanitation.

The soldier's cold word echoed through her mind as she tried to reconnect the lines, but it was too awkward and impossible to do by hand. Not really sure what she should do, Madison hopped off the counter and opened the window above the sink as wide as it could go. She had left the sliding glass door open as well. It wouldn't get rid of *all* the accumulated gas, but it would help.

She had started toward the dining room, her every sense on high alert, when she stopped short and turned back to the counter by the stove. It was stupid, really, but she was remembering all the cheesy horror movies she'd seen over the years, the ones where the teenage girl would go into the creepy house looking for the serial killer, never having anything to defend herself with.

She grabbed the biggest knife from the holder on the counter. Then, her confidence bolstered some, she moved on to the dining room. There was still no sign of anybody, and the house was deathly quiet. That in and of itself was unusual—even when the Arsenaults slept late, they were usually up by now.

At the foot of the stairs she stopped and listened, tempted to call out but thinking again of the stupid teenagers in those movies. She peered up the stairs, and then, holding her knife at the ready, she started up, heart hammering so hard and loud she was certain that the deafening sound of its beating would give her away.

Near the top of the stairs, she crouched and leaned out to check the hallway. The smell of gas was strong up here as well. Seeing and hearing nothing out of the ordinary, she stepped onto the landing and quickly made her way down the hall to her aunt and uncle's room.

She froze just shy of the entrance to their room. The door was ajar, as it usually was when they were sleeping, to keep the cool air from the air conditioner inside yet allow them to hear what was happening in the rest of the house. She reached out a trembling hand to push it open. The door slowly swung inward with a squeak, and she peered inside.

Marty and Ellen were nestled snugly in their beds, sound asleep, the raspy breathing of her uncle over the hum of the AC giving the illusion that everything was as it should be. She approached the bed, reaching down to grab hold of her aunt's leg beneath the comforter. "Aunt Ellen," she whispered, squeezing the woman's leg and giving it a shake. "Aunt Ellen, wake up."

Her aunt remained fast asleep, so Madison turned her attention to her uncle. She set her carving knife down on the nightstand beside a glass of water and shook him with both hands. "Uncle Marty, please wake up."

Her uncle continued to breathe loudly, as if so deeply asleep that her voice couldn't get to him. She reached for the glass of water on the nightstand, preparing to douse her uncle to consciousness.

"I'm afraid that will only make him wet," said a voice from behind her.

Madison let out a yelp of surprise, dropped the

water glass and turning around to face Mason Lovett standing in the doorway. She reacted purely on instinct, grabbing up the knife, holding it tightly in both hands, blade pointed in his direction.

Mason sighed, as if exasperated. "I don't want this to be any more difficult than it has to be," he said, coming into the room.

"Stay away from me," she spat. She didn't want him to see that she was afraid, but the knife shook in her grip. "What are you doing in here—what have you done to them?"

Mason looked down at the pair, sound asleep beneath the covers. "I gave them a shot to put them to sleep. This isn't their fault. It's only fair that they not know what's happening to them."

Mason calmly looked at her, and she became even more terrified. "I'd like to give you that same chance. A shot and then you'll go to sleep. I promise it'll be completely painless."

"You'll give me a shot and then what?" she scoffed. "You'll blow up the house around me? Around my aunt and uncle? Are you out of your friggin' mind?"

Mason then produced a gun from somewhere at his back and pulled back the hammer with a loud click. He pointed the weapon at her sleeping aunt and uncle. "Look, I have a job to do here, and it's going to require me to speed things up a bit, so I'd like you to drop that knife this instant or I'll be forced to put a bullet into Marty and Ellen's skulls."

"You're crazy!" Madison shrieked.

"Drop the knife, Madison," he continued with very little emotion.

Madison couldn't move, but her hands shook so badly it looked like she was trying to cut the air with the knife.

"Fine, which one first?" Mason asked, moving the gun from side to side. "Your aunt or your uncle? I'll let you decide."

"No!" she screamed, tears of frustration and anger, spurred by helplessness, starting to flow down her cheeks.

"Then drop the knife."

Madison finally did as she was told, letting the knife fall to the hardwood floor.

"Now kick it over to me," Mason coolly instructed.

She kicked the blade, and it clattered across the floor.

Mason quickly bent down to pick it up. "Thank you," he said, sliding the long kitchen knife between the waistline of his slacks and his brown leather belt.

Madison had the urge to run, a horrible tingling sensation spreading up and down her legs, but she couldn't bear the thought of leaving her aunt and uncle behind.

"I just want you to know that you're being very adult about this," Mason continued. "And I really appreciate it."

She was speechless, staring at the man in shock, as if he were some creature from another world.

"Now, if you would be so kind as to go to your room." He stepped aside and motioned toward the door with the gun.

Numb, Madison left the room, feeling the strange sensation of having a gun pointed at her. She stopped in the doorway to her room and began to turn.

"Inside," he commanded, a hard poke in the back with the gun's barrel convincing her to move faster. "Sit down on the bed and hold out your arm," he told her.

Madison sat at the edge of her bed, watching as Mason, still pointing the gun at her, reached into his shirt pocket and removed what appeared to be a green plastic vial.

"What's that?" she asked.

He brought the vial to his mouth and pulled off the cap with his teeth, revealing a needle. He spat the cap onto the floor. "I told you I would make this as easy for you as I could," he said, coming toward her. "It's the same stuff I gave your aunt and uncle. You'll be asleep before you know it."

"I'll be dead!" she screamed, rolling backward and flipping herself over the bed to the other side of the room.

"Eventually," Mason agreed, "but you won't feel a thing. Now stop this nonsense before you force me to do something really horrible. I'd hate to put a bullet in one of your kneecaps, or maybe you'd like me to march down the hallway and shoot poor Marty while—"

Madison was distracted by a flurry of movement in her doorway and heard herself gasp as Tom Lovett came into her room.

"Don't worry, Madison," he said as his father whipped around, startled by the sound of his voice. "He wouldn't dare use the gun in here. Too much gas: he'd blow himself to bits as well, and I doubt that's part of his plan."

Madison looked at Tom. There was a sheen of sweat on his brow and his chest was heaving as he worked to catch his breath. She was still so confused by every-thing that had happened, but there was no doubt that she was very relieved Tom had come for her.

"He's right," Mason said, shoving the weapon into the waistband of his pants.

Madison knew what was coming. "Tom, watch out!" she screamed, just as Mason Lovett pulled the knife from his belt and leapt at his son.

Victoria remembered the first time she had seen him, ten years ago, sound asleep as he was carried into the house. He would awaken from his narcoleptic spell and remember it as his home and her as his mother.

She checked the connections on the detonator attached to the natural gas pipe in the basement of her neighbors' home and thought about the life she was being forced to abandon.

There had been another life, one that seemed so long ago, it was almost as if she had dreamed it. She had been a freelance operative, a spy whose only allegiance was to whoever could pay the most.

And Brandon Kavanagh had made her the sweetest of offers.

Victoria stared at the small explosive device, mesmerized by the rhythmic flashing of the green sensor eye, pulsing like a heartbeat. There was another one exactly like it across the street at her home, in her basement, and when the time was right, she would push a button on a tiny transmitter that she carried in her pocket and both homes on Burrows Place would be destroyed in an explosion, and the life she had led until that morning would cease to exist—Victoria Lovett would cease to exist.

It wasn't her real name, but in the line of work she had chosen, the opportunity for other identities often presented itself. She and another member of the illustrious intelligence community had been hired by the Janus Project to be the keepers of a newly developed secret weapon of the highest caliber.

She stepped back from her handiwork, mentally preparing herself for the next phase of the sanitation process. It was easier to think of what she was doing in cold, technical terms like *sanitation*. It sounded so much nicer than murder.

Victoria Lovett's left hip struck a stack of plastic storage boxes, and they tumbled over in her path. The white plastic lids came loose, spilling the contents onto the floor. The mess didn't really matter—it would all be ashes in a matter of minutes—but she found herself bending down to pick it up anyway.

Pictures. The containers had been filled with pictures.

Squatting among other boxes filled with old clothes and holiday decorations, she found herself looking through the photographs.

They were pictures of her neighbors, probably from not long after they were married. The couple looked pretty much the same: Marty had been thinner then, which was to be expected, and Ellen's hair had been much darker, not as much gray. *She should color it,* Victoria casually thought before remembering that hair color wouldn't matter much after she had completed her task here. Victoria dropped back into the reality of her mission with a bone-jarring thud.

She was just about to leave the photographs where they had fallen and find her partner when her eyes caught sight of something. It was a photo of a young Ellen Arsenault in what appeared to be a hospital bed, holding a baby.

Victoria pulled the photo from beneath a pile of others and stared at it. Ellen looked exhausted, dark circles under her eyes, her hair a mess, but there was a smile on her face as she held close the tiny bundle of life. Marty must have taken the picture, she imagined, turning it over. Written in a flowery hand, it said, *Baby Meaghan . . . our daughter. Born 12/22/88.*

There were other photos beneath it: the proud parents with their baby girl, and then it struck her. None of them had been taken in a home; all the pictures had been taken in the hospital, and even though the parents were smiling, there was something in their eyes as they looked into the camera, something sad.

She had never seen any sign of children at the Arsenaults' home.

Still sifting through the photos, Victoria came across newspaper clippings. They were death notices from two daily papers, one from the *Hawthorne Gazette* and the other from the *Boston Globe*. They were dated a few weeks after December 22.

The realization struck her suddenly, shockingly: she had been through the house preparing for sanitization and had seen no evidence that this child had ever existed.

It was strange—the Arsenaults' attempt to forget what had obviously meant so much to them. But Victoria understood completely: she was about to do something very similar.

She would have laughed in the face of anyone who suggested that it was possible for her to have a maternal instinct. Certainly she could pretend—which was exactly what she was supposed to be doing, acting to maintain a cover, solidifying the artificial memory implanted in the boy's mind that she was in fact his mother.

How had it ever come to be that she'd started to believe it as well? She knew it was all a fabrication—Tom wasn't a child, he was a weapon of mass destruction capable of the most devastating acts of violence. But then why did carrying out her duty suddenly feel so difficult?

Victoria recalled the first time she had seen the

other personality activated. It had been a demonstration in the presence of their employer, Brandon Kavanagh, before their cover had been established. He'd explained the process to her with a certain amount of excitement—a microchip had been surgically implanted in the cerebral cortex of the child's brain, and once stimulated by a satellite transmission, it would trigger a narcoleptic seizure and initiate the transfer of personas.

It had been chilling to watch the little boy through the two-way glass who, though he had moments before shied away from the automatic pistol that had been placed before him by an attendant, now picked up the weapon, dismantling it and putting it back together in record time.

Victoria still hadn't quite figured out why Kavanagh had given the boy's other personality a southern drawl. She imagined that he derived some kind of twisted amusement from it.

She dropped the pictures and glared resentfully at the explosive device flashing on the gas pipe behind her. There had always been a possibility it would have to end this way, but a part of her had hoped it wouldn't.

Mason Lovett had to wonder if he had the skills to kill this boy.

He leapt toward the startled youth, ready to make his knife strike as damaging as possible.

Of course he'd heard the stories, how the Tyler Garrett side of the persona was the perfect weapon, how he had been programmed to kill with a cold, calculating efficiency. *Blah, blah, blah, blah.*

None of that mattered at the moment. Mason had been in enough battles throughout his career to know that it usually came down to who was the most aggressive—who wanted to live the most. And he definitely did not want to die.

Faced with a similar situation ten years or so ago, he would have put his money on the other guy. He'd been a wreck, a shell of the man he'd once been. He had done some things in his life—despicable things that he wasn't proud of but could always justify in the name of survival. But he had reached a point when he couldn't close his eyes without seeing the blood-spattered faces of those who fallen before his own need for survival. The life of a mercenary was killing him, but it was all he had ever known. Then Brandon Kavanagh had called with an offer that at first horrified him—*me as the guardian of child?*—and then fascinated him. The innocence of a child masking the identity of a killer; it was disturbingly brilliant. Thus Mason Lovett had been born.

Mason studied his opponent as he attacked—the way he stood, the look of fear in his eyes. This wasn't a killing machine; it was a scared boy.

It made what he had to do all the easier.

He thrust the long blade toward Tom's chest. This would be a killing strike, and he felt no remorse. This was what it always came down to: it was either you or them.

Mason anticipated the sensation that was to follow his thrust, the vibration that would travel up through the metal of the blade, into the handle, and into his arm—the feeling of flesh pierced and the razor-sharp edge of a blade grazing across bone as the point of the weapon sought the pulsing muscular organ behind the rib cage that was the human heart. It was a sensation he had felt before and one that he was ready to feel again.

Somehow the knife blade missed the boy's heart—missed the boy altogether, actually. Tom had darted to one side at the last-possible moment. Mason spun around to the right, slashing at where he imagined Tom to be. It was unusual for him not to hit his mark on the first try, and it proved how rusty he had become as babysitter to Kavanagh's prized science project.

His second attack missed as well, the knife blade gouging the wooden door frame and part of the wall.

Mason spun again, knife poised, prepared to strike for a third and final time.

Kavanagh had been very specific during the briefing at the start of the mission. If Tom ever realized his true purpose, the operation was to be aborted at once. The boy's potential for mayhem was high, and he must never be given the opportunity to operate unchecked.

And now, as Mason stared into the eyes of the boy who once believed him to be his father, he saw something that hadn't been there before. He saw a cruelty reflected in Tom's gaze. These were eyes no longer fooled by the illusions of the world.

They were eyes that had seen beneath the mask.

It was as if some kind of slow-mo button had been pushed inside his brain, the moment like still pictures taken in succession being slowly flipped to give the impression of movement.

His father was trying to kill him.

No. Not my father, Tom corrected himself, *a handler, somebody who couldn't give two shits about me. This is not my father.*

Tom watched in horror as his father—*his handler*—jumped at him, carving knife in hand. As long as he had known the man, Tom had never seen him move this quickly. Even the expression he wore was completely foreign. It was as if he was someone else entirely, a killer hiding inside his father's body.

They were acting, dumb ass. You had to believe they were your parents if the operation was going to work.

The knife was closer now, aimed at Tom's heart, and he still hadn't decided what he was going to do, though the choices were simple. He could stand there and be stabbed through the chest, bringing an end to this whole nightmarish scenario, or he could move out of the way, live a little longer, and give *Dad* another chance at killing him.

And then there's the other option.

Tom had pretty much had his fill of the strange presence he could feel sharing his body. He could have easily gone with choice number one just so all this would finally be over. Yeah, he'd be dead, but at least it would be done with.

The blade was even closer now and Tom could see the details of the kitchen knife, nothing fancy, but definitely sharp. *Do I really want to die?*

There is another choice, he was reminded. What had the guy back at the hotel in West Virginia—Tremain—what had he called it when the two sides came together?

Unification.

Tom watched the knife as it moved toward him

with wicked precision. He imagined that he could hear the blade as it sliced through the air, sounding an awful lot like a jet fighter dropping down to zero in on its target.

If unification was to happen, he was going to have to let down the barriers, let himself flow into the assassin and the assassin into him.

We'd make one helluva team, he heard Tyler Garrett say.

The knife blade glinted seductively as it crossed the point of no return. He'd be killed and then Mason would go about his business; no one would be the wiser.

What a horrible shame, people would say, *those poor families dying like that.*

Tom glanced across the room where Madison was; she gave him a pleading look.

The image of a large plate glass window suddenly appeared inside his mind, a window separating a world of calm from a raging storm. Slowly the window began to open, the elemental fury outside the barrier pounding against the obstruction, desperate to enter. The glass trembled furiously and then exploded inward, incapable of holding back the might of the storm.

Tom gasped, his insides flushed with liquid fire, and he knew—his body knew—what it was truly capable of.

The blade was mere inches from its destination, and Tom willed himself from its path. He felt like he'd never felt before; it was what he imagined it would be like behind the wheel of a sports car, the engine revving powerfully beneath its hood.

He felt good. Like he would never have an attack of narcolepsy again—like he would never need to sleep again.

From the corner of his eye Tom saw his attacker's reaction, body stopping its forward momentum into the upstairs hallway, pivoting around with the knife for another chance at ending his life.

Tom jumped back farther into the room, the knife's edge gouging the door frame and leaving a deep gash across the wallpaper.

The handler spun around then, ready to follow through, but he paused as he stared at Tom, studying him, studying his eyes. "Where are your glasses?" he asked in that fatherly tone, making the boy's flesh crawl. "You should learn to take better care of your things, Tom."

"Don't talk to me that way," Tom spat. "You don't even know me anymore."

Mason feinted a lunge to the left but went right, and Tom saw his opportunity. He stepped in close, avoiding the knife blade again but directing a blow to

Mason's kidney, causing him to cry out as he doubled over in pain. Tom jumped back but not fast enough. The knife caught him on the upper arm, easily cutting across his T-shirt and the soft flesh beneath.

He winced, his hand going to the gash in his arm, and he felt the flow of blood beneath his fingers.

"First blood," Mason growled, showing Tom the knife and how beads of his blood now dappled the steel.

And Tom felt all the pain, rage, and fear that he was experiencing at the moment channeled through his body distilled into an inner power that made him oblivious to the situation at hand. There was only winning and losing, the victor and the vanquished.

"Think of it as a present," Tom snapped, lunging at the man who had hurt him in so many more ways than with just the slash of a knife.

Mason jabbed with his weapon again, but Tom was ready, grabbing hold of his wrist and applying pressure, twisting it painfully to one side. Mason shrieked, and the knife fell from his hand to the floor.

Weaponless, Mason lashed out. He kneed Tom's side, following through with an elbow between the shoulder blades that nearly collapsed him.

Tom grabbed hold of Mason's shirt, pulling himself up and driving the crown of his head into the man's chin. Mason stumbled backward in a daze, falling into a dresser, knocking over bottles of perfume before sliding to the floor as Tom leapt on top of him.

Bloody memories of numerous fights surged into his consciousness. It had always looked so clean in the movies, like a choreographed dance number, a ballet of violence—graceful in a twisted sort of way, but in fact it was something altogether different. It was ugly, brutal, two individuals reduced to savagery.

Tom didn't remember ever having been here before, to this primal place, but his other half . . . it reveled in the freedom, the simplicity.

The two struggled with each other, rolling around the bedroom floor, punching and clawing at each other. It had all come down to the most basic of needs.

The need to survive.

Mason planted a foot beneath Tom's midsection and pushed away, hurling him backward across the room. He crashed back against the closet door, the force of the impact making his head spin. Giving his head a shake to clear away the static, he was ready to continue the fight. But Mason Lovett was already at him, having retrieved the knife from the floor, the glinting metal sweeping through the air on a course with his side.

Tom's mind raced, a million and one scenarios on how to survive this latest attack playing out in the blink of an eye.

"This is going to hurt me more than it hurts you," Mason grunted.

And the words froze Tom solid, because it wasn't the voice of a government agent he heard then but the voice of the man who had raised him, comforted him when he was sick. This was the voice of the man Tom had thought loved him.

The voice of a father.

And it tore him up inside, doing more damage than any knife possibly could. The father he had known—the father whom he had cared for and who had loved him as a son was dead now, killed in the most bizarre of accidents.

The blade grazed his side in a searing flash of pure agony, and he twisted away from its bite, throwing himself across the room to escape it. Spots of exploding color blossomed before his eyes as he attempted to get back to his feet.

"It's for your own good, Tom," Mason continued, slightly out of breath, coming toward him to finish the job.

Tom's legs trembled as he anticipated the handler's next attack. He could feel the warmth of blood leaking from the wound in his side, and he wondered how much punishment his body could take before it shut down.

Madison sprang from the corner of the room, jumping on top of the bed and across Mason's path, throwing her full weight against the knife-wielding man, knocking him back against the wall.

"Get out, Tom!" she screamed, focusing her attention on relieving Mason of his weapon. "Get help!"

Mason savagely backhanded her, and she fell to the floor in a broken heap.

"Didn't your father ever teach you not to hit girls?" Tom growled as he drove his fist into the man's face, knocking his head back against the wall. Tom followed through with a second punch, putting everything he could into the blow.

Mason's body went limp as Tom punched him again and again. His knuckles were torn and bloody, but still he continued to rain blows down on the man, never giving him the opportunity to recover. All the while Tyler Garrett was strangely silent, but Tom could sense he was there—could sense his influence with every bloody punch.

The knife fell from Mason's hand as Tom's fist landed on him one final time, driving him to the floor. Tom stumbled back, suddenly dizzy and out of breath, staring down at the man whose face now looked like raw meat.

Tom's eyes dropped to the knife lying on the floor,

and he went for it, grabbing it up and holding it tightly in his hand. He looked at his unconscious father—his enemy—struggling with the urge to end this conflict once and for all, to take the man's life. And it was a battle he nearly lost to the bloodlust, but he was saved on hearing the soft sound of Madison's moans.

Suppressing his rage, Tom tossed the butcher knife, embedding the blade in the wall across the room where it could do no harm, and went to her.

"Hey," he said, helping her to rise. "Are you all right?"

Her lip was swollen and bloody as she looked at him, carefully studying his face. "I could ask you the same thing," she said, wincing as she attempted to smile.

"I'm as good as can be expected," he said, just as somebody seemed to tilt the room to one side and he stumbled. Madison grabbed hold of him, planting her feet to keep him standing.

"Well, maybe not that good," he mumbled, trying to remain upright.

"We have to get out of here," she said, steering him toward the door. "My aunt and uncle are unconscious in their bedroom; we can—"

Madison's words abruptly stopped, her and Tom's move to freedom cut short by the sight of Mason Lovett standing in the doorway.

"You're going nowhere," the man slurred, swaying on his feet. He had retrieved his gun from the waistband of his pants and was pointing it at them. "None of us is going anywhere."

Mason's face was a bloody mask, one of his eyes swollen shut.

"I know you won't use that in here," Tom said, putting himself in front of Madison. "The gunfire will ignite the gas—you'll be killed too."

Mason smiled then, a horrible smile, what teeth remained stained with blood. "I've decided I'm willing to take that risk. Are you?"

Tom tensed, and just as he saw Mason's finger twitch on the pistol's trigger, he heard the strangest of sounds. It was like a tennis ball being thrown off a wall, and he watched as Mason's one good eye rolled up into the back of his head. He pitched forward into the room, revealing Victoria Lovett, heavy plumber's wrench in hand, standing in the doorway.

The expression on Victoria's face reminded Tom of shattering glass, a steely resolve suddenly disintegrating into an expression of overwhelming grief. But it was there for only the briefest of moments as she quickly looked away from him and down the hall.

"You need to get out of here right now," she said,

looking back again with that fleeting shadow of sadness. "The gas is building up and—"

"I don't understand," he said. "Why are you doing this?"

"There's no time for that." She tossed the wrench onto the bed, moving down the hall toward the Arsenaults' bedroom. "You need to get them up and out before the explosives detonate."

"Explosives?" Madison cried.

"The ones I set in the basements here and next door," Victoria clarified.

There wasn't a moment to lose. Marty and Ellen were shaken from their drug-induced stupor and helped from the room. The drug given to them by Mason must have been wearing off, and the two were able to be guided trancelike out into the hall and toward the staircase.

"Is there a fire?" Marty asked, sounding like he'd had one too many drinks.

Madison explained that yes, there was indeed a fire, and they had to leave the house as quickly as possible. The two didn't argue, following her down the stairs.

Tom leaned against the door frame, his head swimming from the simple exertion.

"You're hurt." The only mother he had ever known came to his side.

"Why are you helping us?" he asked, avoiding her touch.

She didn't answer, bearing some of his weight as she helped him from the room and toward the stairs.

"Let's just say I've had a change of heart," she said as they carefully made their way down the staircase to the small foyer.

The door had been left open, and Tom felt the air from outside flowing in to dissipate the powerful aroma of gas.

"Go," she said, pushing him out the door onto the front porch.

He stopped, turning around. "Where are you going?" he asked her.

"Go," she said again, and he watched as she removed what looked to be a car starter from inside her pocket.

"You can't," he said, again feeling his reality start to crumble all around him. "I need you," he croaked. "I . . . I can't lose everything."

For a moment it seemed as if his pleas might have actually had an effect, and she stepped toward the doorway—toward him—but the disfigured form of Mason Lovett suddenly appeared at the bottom of the stairs, grabbing her from behind and drawing her back inside.

"No!" Tom screamed, throwing himself toward the house. Victoria struggled with her husband—her partner—and Tom watched as she reached out to grab hold of the door, slamming it closed in his face.

He tried to get it open but couldn't, and then he felt hands on him and an urgent voice spoke in his ear as he was dragged backward, away from the house.

"Come on!" Madison cried as she hauled him down the steps and onto the front lawn, just as the world exploded in a blinding flash of fire and thunder.

It was like the sound of the ocean inside a seashell, except for the ringing. He didn't recall ever having heard ringing when listening to a seashell.

Tom lifted his face up from the cool, damp grass of the front lawn and looked around. Bits of flaming debris lay scattered; the heavy aroma of burning wood, plastic, and other pungent smells choked the air.

The gash in his side throbbed as he started to stand, and he was positive that he'd let loose an audible yelp, but he couldn't hear it over the sound of the ringing in his ears.

Tom managed to get to his feet and turned in the direction of where his house should be. It was gone, as was the house next door to it; all that remained were the stone foundations and piles of burning wreckage that had once been the two homes on Burrows Place.

"Tom?"

Over the ringing he thought he heard his name and pulled his attention away from the rubble to see Madison limping toward him.

His heart skipped a beat at the sight of her. Even though her clothes were filthy and her face was covered in soot and drying blood, she was still an amazing sight.

He met her halfway, and she fell into his arms. They held each other for what felt like hours, and by the time they let go, the noise in his ears had started to subside. Far off in the distance he could hear sirens wailing and guessed it would only be a matter of time before the police and the fire department arrived. For a moment he wondered how he was going to explain what had happened.

Honestly, Officer, I really am an assassin for a secret organization.

Tom squinted through the billowing smoke toward the top of the street and caught the yellow glow of headlights.

Marty and Ellen had noticed them as well, getting to their bare feet in their pajamas on the other side of the blackened foundation that was once their home. Marty waved at the four black sports utility vehicles that emerged from the thick smoke.

"Who are they?" Madison asked, a hint of caution creeping into her voice.

Tom didn't answer, watching as two of the vehicles parked, blocking the street, while the other two pulled up in front of them.

A nervous sweat broke out on Tom's brow; he didn't need the senses of an assassin to know that something wasn't right.

Men dressed in dark suits and wearing sunglasses emerged from the vehicles, circling around to protect a man who was last to exit.

Tom had tensed, ready for another fight, when he realized that he recognized the man.

"It's good to see you still alive, Tom," Christian Tremain said, walking toward him. The men surrounding Tremain reached inside their coats for their guns, and Tom prepared for the worst.

"Stand down," Tremain ordered, and the men withdrew their hands, eyeing each other nervously. God only knew what they'd heard about him—what they knew he was capable of.

Tremain stepped closer. "I'm truly sorry about this," he said, looking at the burning wreckage of the two homes, and for some strange reason, Tom actually believed him. "I wish we could have figured out your location sooner."

"Who are you?" Madison suddenly asked. "Who is this, Tom?" she asked him, not waiting for Tremain to answer.

"He's the man I was sent to kill," Tom said flatly.

Taking hold of his arm and moving closer, Madison continued to stare at Tremain, studying his appearance. He was dressed in a three-piece suit, a tie spotted with stains, and a wrinkled trench coat that looked like he might have slept in it. It wasn't a look that inspired much confidence, but then again, it was all Tom had at the moment.

"I offered to help you before, Tom, and the offer still stands," the man stated. "Come with us and we'll do everything we can to help you understand what has been done to you."

Tom turned his head to focus on the remains of his home—at the wreckage that seemed to embody what had happened to his life. A single person had done this to him; one man had taken it all away.

"I want to meet the guy responsible for this," he said, tearing his sight away from the devastation. "I'll go with you, but you have to promise me that I'll get a chance to meet Brandon Kavanagh."

Tremain nodded slowly. "I'm sure that can be arranged," he said, gesturing for Tom to accompany him toward the waiting vehicles. "A team has been dispatched to take him into custody, and I'm certain that after he's processed, we'll be able to arrange for you to—"

"So that I can kill him," Tom stated coldly, a little startled by the words that left his mouth but meaning them just the same. He doubted that the old Tom would have been able to go through with such an act, but the old Tom wasn't around anymore.

"Why don't we discuss this back at headquarters?" Tremain said as he opened the passenger door of the SUV for them. "We'll get you patched up, and then we'll talk about Kavanagh and what he's been up to."

Tom agreed with a nod, helping Madison up into the vehicle before getting in himself. Tremain closed the door, leaving them alone in the backseat of the SUV.

Tom watched through the front windshield as Tremain talked with his agents, discovering with distant surprise that he was able to read their lips. He, Madison, and the Arsenaults were going to be taken back to home base—to the headquarters of something called the Pandora Group, in Washington, D.C., for debriefing. He had never been to Washington—that he could remember, anyway. He watched the agents herd the still-confused Marty and Ellen into the back of another of the vehicles.

"Tom?" he heard Madison say, and he looked into her eyes. He wanted to smile at her, to reassure her that everything was going to be all right, but he just couldn't find it in himself.

"What you said to Tremain?" she said. "What *you* said about killing the man responsible for doing this . . . Was it you, Tom? Was it you talking or . . ."

"It was me," he said, looking away from her and out the window, past the Pandora agents discussing their next course of action to the smoldering remains of what had once been his home—what was left of his life. "It was all me."

Brandon Kavanagh stepped over the body of the dead Pandora Group operative on his way out of his office. He had said that his name was Sommerset and that he had been ordered to bring Kavanagh in for questioning.

Like hell he was.

Kavanagh left his office and never once looked back.

He had known they'd be coming for him once they had finally put all the pieces of the puzzle together. *I wonder what finally gave it away?* he pondered, stepping through a bullet-riddled security door. *Could it have been the attempt on Tremain's life?* He smirked. *Of course it was, but it wouldn't have fallen apart so quickly if something hadn't gone wrong with Sleeper One.*

A flash of anger coursed through him then, and he quickly suppressed it. There was no need to get upset.

He would just have to review the data and determine what had gone wrong, making sure that it never happened again. There was far too much riding on his future plans for this to stop him. What was it his grandmother used to say when things looked particularly grim? *"Think of it as just a bump in the road."*

There were more dead Pandora agents lying in pools of blood along the hallway, and he did exactly as his grandmother had instructed, stepping over the bumps to move forward with his journey. She would have been so proud to learn that he'd taken her lessons to heart.

The door at the end of the battle-scarred corridor began to open, and he removed the gun that he had used to murder Agent Sommerset from inside his coat pocket.

His head of security, Noah Wells, stepped through the doorway into the hall, a smile on his usually cruel features.

"Don't shoot," he said dryly, raising his arms in mock surrender.

Noah had been with Kavanagh from the beginning, and Kavanagh doubted that there was anyone in the world more loyal. It was like having a really smart pit bull at your side at all times.

Kavanagh returned the weapon to his pocket as

Wells held open the door for him to exit. "All members of the Pandora security team sent to close us down have been dealt with," Wells said casually as Kavanagh passed by him into the lobby. "It's not pretty out here."

And he was correct. It looked like a major offensive had occurred there: dead bodies of Pandora operatives as well as his own security team littered the floor, their blood mingling as it coagulated on the Italian marble. The project's receptionist, Karen, lay facedown on her desk, phone clutched in a blood-spattered hand. Only here did he allow himself to experience the slightest pangs of emotion.

"That's too bad," he said, looking from Karen's body to Wells. "She made an excellent cup of coffee."

Wells nodded. "Yep, she certainly did. Not bad on the eyes either."

Kavanagh hated to leave his facility. They had done good work here, made the kind of advances that allowed them to be where they were today. He had overseen the transmittal of all pertinent data to their new base of operation himself, wiping all hard drives clean with a small electromagnetic detonation as soon as they had given up their bounty. Pandora would have to get their information from somewhere else if they planned on continuing their pursuit of him, as he was certain they would.

"This is it, then," Kavanagh said. He looked around the lobby one last time, for old times' sake, and then headed for the door.

It was beautiful outside, and he breathed in a lungful of West Virginia summer air, replacing the stench of gunfire and blood.

A sleek black helicopter waited in the parking lot, its blades beginning to turn as the two men emerged from the building.

"Do you want to do the honors?" Wells asked, holding out the transmitter that would detonate multiple explosive devices placed all around the building, eliminating any stray evidence that the Janus Project had ever existed.

"No thank you," Kavanagh said as he descended the steps of the former psychiatric facility. "I know how much pleasure you get from blowing things up."

Wells chuckled as he pointed the transmitter and hit the button. "I'm just a big kid at heart," he said. The muffled *whoomph*ing sounds of powerful explosions could be heard from inside.

Kavanagh glanced over his shoulder as he crossed the lot, catching sight of the facility's windows exploding outward, tongues of orange flame reaching out to lap the sky.

"Have you decided what you're going to do about

Sleeper One?" Wells asked as they walked, crouching slightly the closer they got to the helicopter and its whirling rotors. "I can't imagine the boy being in the Pandora Group's custody will be good for us."

Kavanagh considered the question for a moment. "At first I looked at that as a real problem," he responded, waiting as Wells opened the chopper door for him. "But then I remembered a little something my grandmother used to say."

Wells chuckled as he slid into the seat beside his employer.

"Why are you laughing?" Kavanagh asked as he strapped himself in.

"It's nothing, just that your grandmother must have been a fine woman."

Kavanagh tapped the seat in front of him, signaling to the pilot that it was time to go. "She was a ruthless bitch," he answered in kind. "But she understood how things worked and how things could be twisted to work specifically for you."

Wells gazed out the window as the chopper rose vertically into the air. "And what would she have said about this situation—the situation with Sleeper One?"

Kavanagh smiled, remembering the old woman, nothing but skin and bones, confined to her wheelchair. God, how she had scared him.

"She would have said, Brandon, when life gives you lemons, you make lemonade."

Wells laughed as they flew over the burning building that once housed the secret operation known as the Janus Project.

"I'm going to make lemonade, Wells," Kavanagh said as he closed his eyes to think about the future. "Lots and lots of lemonade."

END OF BOOK ONE

Acknowledgments

My loving thanks to LeeAnne and Mulder, for never giving up on me, and to Christopher Golden for always having the time to listen to my nonsense.

And extra special thanks to Eloise Flood for saving the Sleeper from eternal rest, and Margaret "Madge" Wright for keeping all the facts straight.

My gratitude also to Mom & Dad Sniegoski, David Kraus, Ken Curtis, Kim & Abby, David Carroll, Jon & Flo, Bob & Pat, John Wallace, Jean Eddy, Pete Donaldson, Jay Sanders, Tim Cole and the Brotherhood of Evil, Eric Powell, Don Kramer, Greg Skopis, and Steve the Barber who keeps me looking so gosh darn handsome.

Thank you one and all.

—T.S.

Turn the page for a sneak peek at
Part II of the Sleeper Conspiracy,

SLEEPER AGENDA

Agent Abernathy's fist connected with the side of Tom's face, snapping his head violently to the right. Tom's mouth was suddenly filled with the coppery taste of blood and his ears rang loudly. He stumbled back away from his assailant.

"I don't understand how kicking my ass is going to help anything," he complained as he removed the padded headgear and looked to Tremain, who stood on the sidelines of the workout room, sipping coffee from a plastic cup.

"We need to see how much of the Tyler persona has been assimilated into your own," he said. "And if new information can be accessed when it's needed."

Tom shook his head. He was tired of all the testing and prodding that had become his life since arriving at the Pandora facility. "You already know what I can do," he said, exasperation creeping into his voice.

Tremain had been there the day Tom had survived the attack by a Janus assault squad and his own parents.

Tom felt his rage surge. No, those people weren't his parents—they never had been, and the sooner he accepted that, the better off he'd be. No matter how many times he thought about their betrayal, he couldn't bring himself to let them go. There were still so many good memories.

But then, those were likely lies as well, implants, false memories to make him believe his life was real.

All so they could hide a killer inside his head.

Tremain took another sip of his coffee as two more agents dressed in workout gear entered the gym and joined Abernathy.

"Humor us, Tom," Tremain said. "Just spar with them. They won't hurt you."

Abernathy grinned and winked at Tom as he slowly approached the three agents.

"It's not me that I'm worried about," Tom grumbled, placing the padded gear back on his head.

"So how do you want to do this?" he asked, standing in front of the men, focusing his attention on Agent Abernathy. "Want to crack me in the face again to remind me where we left off?"

The man laughed. "That was just a love tap, kid,"

he said, punching the knuckles of his red padded gloves together. "Thought you were something special—guess I was wrong."

The other agents chuckled, and Tom felt something within him snap. Abernathy didn't even see it coming. Tom reacted instantaneously, smashing his fist across the agent's handsome, grinning face. He stumbled back toward his buddies, who caught him and saved him from falling.

Tom punched his own gloved fists together, imitating Abernathy. "Special enough to kick your ass, I guess," he said.

Abernathy recovered fast, shaking off the punch and coming at Tom straight on, fists raised to give him the beating of his life.

Tom had planted his feet and was waiting for that spark of inspiration that would show him how to react when he heard Tremain yell from the sidelines.

"All of you, take him down—hard, if you have to."

Tom shot him a quick, surprised glance, and Tremain raised his coffee cup in a mock salute. Tom turned back to the three agents in time to see Abernathy's fist careening toward his face, and suddenly his brain somehow slowed down the action. He moved his head from the path of the punch, feeling a breeze as the leather-clad fist sailed past, dangerously close.

Then Tom stepped in, grabbing hold of Abernathy's arm at the elbow, bending it sharply in a direction it wasn't meant to go. He heard the agent hiss in pain and applied even more pressure, forcing him to choose between a broken arm or dropping to his knees.

"What's it gonna be?" Tom asked, feeling the man begin to struggle, but then common sense prevailed, and Abernathy lowered himself to the floor.

Tom pushed the man away and turned to the other two agents, who now circled him. He didn't know their names, but he had seen them around the Pandora facility. They were stereotypical special agents—square-jawed, painfully serious, and in excellent physical condition.

Just two more pieces of meat that need to be cut down to size, he thought with a weird tingle of fear and excitement as he attacked his opponents, not a doubt in his mind that he would soon be the only one standing.

Well, I'll be damned, Tremain thought, drinking from his cup, afraid that if he took his eyes from the scene, he just might miss something.

Deacons and Stanley attacked together, and if Tremain had been a betting man, he wouldn't have given a second thought to who the victors of this little rumble would be. After all, a kid, weighing, what, one-twenty, one-thirty at the absolute most, shouldn't have stood a chance against two former CIA operatives.

The kid moved like a blur, taking out Stanley—the larger of the two agents—first. He seemed to defy gravity as he leapt into the air to deliver a spinning kick that nearly took the agent's head off. Tremain thought that Deacons might have gained the upper hand when he grabbed Tom from behind and pinned the kid's arms to his sides. But the advantage was only temporary.

Tom was able to squirm around in the agent's grasp; then he drove his forehead into the man's chin, forcing him to lose his grip.

Tremain felt the chill of dread at the base of his neck. The boy was smiling as he delivered an open-palm strike to the center of Deacons's chest. The man stumbled back, gasping for breath, and fell to the floor.

That wasn't a challenge for him at all, Tremain realized. There could have been four more agents in the room and he doubted it would have mattered. The kid hadn't even broken a sweat. But that was what Tremain needed to see. He had to know how much of Tyler Garrett had been absorbed into Tom's psyche. And maybe—just maybe—he could access the information that would lead them to Kavanagh.

Tom was standing in the center of the gym, his head

slowly moving from side to side as he sized up his adversaries. The three Pandora agents were gradually recovering, slowly rising to their feet, looking a bit rough around the edges.

"Is that all you've got?" he heard Tom ask them, swaying gently. His eyes darted between each of the agents, recording their every movement as he readied himself to spring into action.

Fascinating, Tremain caught himself thinking as he watched the boy. He immediately stifled his admiration; these skills had been created by Kavanagh for the sake of greed and destruction.

The agents had given up, raising their hands in a sign of submission as they began to walk away. Tremain, believing the session to be over, headed for a nearby trash can to dispose of his empty cup. The sounds of violence distracted him, and he turned back to the center of the room, stunned to find Tom attacking the agents with abandon.

Deacons lay on the ground, unmoving, blood from his mouth and nose forming a puddle beneath his head.

Stanley was attempting to get away, running in a crouch toward the exit, but Tom was right behind him—a predator on the hunt. With what appeared to be little effort, Tom sprang into the air, propelling himself toward the back of the fleeing agent. The heel of his sneaker connected with the back of Stanley's head, sending him sprawling, unconscious, to the floor.

"Tom! Stop!" Tremain hollered, but the boy didn't seem to hear.

He was already moving toward Abernathy, the last of his adversaries. The agent was standing, ready for the attack, and there was fear in the seasoned veteran's eyes.

"Tom, stop this right now! They've had enough!"

Tom sprang at Abernathy, raining a flurry of blows on his face. The Pandora agent was driven to his knees under the relentless onslaught, his hands trying to protect his bloody face. Tom grabbed him by the hair, pulling back his head, preparing to deliver a blow to the man's throat.

A killing strike.

Slowly Tremain approached them. "Tom," he said quietly, and again there was no response.

"Tyler, stand down!" the director suddenly bellowed, his voice echoing around the gymnasium.

The boy let Abernathy's limp body drop to the floor. He glared at Tremain, and for a moment the director felt like he was in the presence of someone else entirely.

"My name is Tom," the boy said through gritted teeth, then turned on his heels and stormed from the gym.

But as Tremain stared at his three fallen agents, he had to wonder if that was altogether true.

Madison Fitzgerald was leaving the Pandora Group, returning to her mother's home in Chicago.

She didn't have much to pack, certainly not enough to warrant the large duffel bag they had given her. *A shopping bag would have been more than enough*, she thought, double-checking the dresser drawers. Most of the things she'd had at her aunt and uncle's house had been lost in the explosion that had destroyed their home as well as the Lovetts' next door—*or whoever the hell they were*.

Madison felt a twinge of lingering fear as she thought about how she'd almost died.

She went through the bag resting on her bed in an attempt to distract herself—a few T-shirts, jeans, some sweatpants, mostly provided by the Pandora Group.

Her aunt and uncle had been brought here too, but they'd quickly been relocated. Along with her parents, they'd been fed a story about Tom's family being part of some radical anti-government group planning terrorist acts and told that the explosions had been caused by bomb-making equipment stored in their basement. They'd all bought it, but Madison knew otherwise. The truth was still so hard to process, though . . . the fact that she'd fallen for someone harder than she'd ever fallen before. And that someone, Tom, happened to have a second personality who was a cold-blooded killer.

She shook the thought from her mind and went to the bathroom to get her soap and shampoo. Catching a glimpse of herself in the mirror over the sink, she stopped, staring at her reflection. Before all this her biggest problem had been her parents' divorce. It almost felt like she wasn't even the same person anymore. Madison stuffed her shampoo into the duffel with her clothes and sighed, sitting down heavily on the bed.

Just that morning she'd gone through something called a debriefing. She'd sat at a table and been given page after page of documents to sign, each of them telling her what she could and couldn't talk about to the outside world unless she wanted to spend some time in jail.

Who would believe me anyway? she wondered, zipping the bag closed.

Madison looked at the clock on the dresser and saw that it was almost noon. They'd be coming soon to drive her to the airport, the beginning of her journey home.

Home.

Her mind raced. Was it possible to go back to a

normal life? Did she even want to? But what choice did she have—they certainly wouldn't let her hang around the Pandora Group.

The digital clock flashed 12:00, and she stood, grabbing her bag and slinging it over her shoulder. She was surprised that no one had arrived at her door. She'd sort of been expecting Tom.

She crossed the room, trying not to think about why he hadn't come to say goodbye. Just as she reached for the knob, there was a knock. She opened the door and found herself looking into Tom Lovett's gorgeous eyes. His hair was wild, his cheeks flushed.

"Thank God you're still here," he said, slightly out of breath. "I was in the gym—lost track of the time. I was afraid I was gonna miss you."

He smiled at her then, and she had no choice but to smile back.

How could she ever live without Tom Lovett?

Tom leaned against the door frame and sighed with relief. She was still here.

"When I saw the time, I started to freak—"

"I would've waited," she interrupted, slipping her hands into the back pockets of her jeans.

He smiled. *God, she's beautiful.* It still knocked him out every time he saw her.

"So you're going, huh?" he said, silently cursing himself for sounding lame.

Madison nodded. "Back to the old homestead," she said, avoiding his eyes. "Mom's still there, but Dad moved out a couple of months ago."

"It must be sort of weird, so much has changed," Tom said.

"Yeah, but it'll still be home. I guess that's lucky."

Tom secretly envied her at that moment, having something to return to. Everything he had known—his past, his home, and family, everything that had defined him as a person—was gone.

Everything except Madison, and now . . .

"So are they going to keep you here?" she asked, her striking green eyes finally meeting his.

Tom shrugged. "I guess. They want to do more tests and stuff."

"Guess they got what they needed from me," she said, smiling sadly.

"You shouldn't be here anyway," he told her, shaking his head. "This isn't the place for you."

"It isn't for you either," Madison said. "I'm worried about you."

He smiled. "Don't be. I'll be fine. There's still a lot I have to learn about myself and about what's been done to me."

feel bad about leaving you," she repeated, again refusing to look at him. "We've been through so much."

Tom swallowed, his heart racing. All he wanted to do was hold her, bring her close, kiss her the way he'd wanted to since the first time he'd seen her. There'd just been so much happening, and then here at the facility, there were always the guards around. . . . His gaze flicked out to the hallway, and he saw it was clear. He stepped forward, about to reach out to her, when Madison suddenly turned and ducked back inside her room. He stood in the doorway, watching as she went to the bedside table and opened the drawer. She removed a pad of paper and a pen and began to write.

"Here," she said, handing him the folded piece of paper.

"What's this?" he asked, before opening it.

"My e-mail address and phone number," she answered.

"Cool." He read the address, already committing it to memory. "They haven't given me e-mail access yet—"

"Well, as soon as you get it, write to me," she finished for him.

He noticed that she was looking at something over his shoulder and turned to see a Pandora agent standing there, waiting.

"Looks like your escort has arrived," he said quietly, disappointment knotting in his stomach.

"Looks that way." She reached down to pick up her bag.

Tom felt a wave of panic. He didn't want her to leave—didn't want to say goodbye to his only comfort.

The agent glanced at his watch. "You really need to go," Tom said, trying to sound nonchalant. "You don't want to miss your flight."

Madison looked over to her escort and held up a finger asking for one more minute. The man nodded but only took a couple of steps aside, still watching them.

"This is it," she said, and all Tom could do was nod stiffly as he wrestled with emotions he could barely contain.

She dropped the bag to the floor and threw her arms around him in a hug. Tom wrapped his own arms around her, holding her tightly. Her body melted into his.

"You take care of yourself, Tom Lovett," Madison whispered against his neck, her voice shaking with emotion.

Tom took a deep breath and gently pushed her away. "You'd better get going." He inclined his head toward the guard. "He's waiting."

Madison kept her hands clasped around his neck, and he stared into her bright green eyes for another moment. His eyes traveled down to her lips, and again he thought about kissing her, not even caring anymore about the guard standing there. But he hesitated, and suddenly she was picking up her bag and, without another word, walking away.